A BAD DAY FOR VOODOO

A BAD DAY FOR VOODOO

JEFF STRAND

sourcebooks
fire

Published by Sourcebooks Fire, an imprint of Sourcebooks, Inc.

P.O. Box 4410, Naperville, Illinois 60567-4410

(630) 961-3900

Fax: (630) 961-2168

teenfire.sourcebooks.com

Library of Congress Cataloging-in-Publication data is on file with the publisher.

Printed and bound in the United States of America.

VP 10 9 8 7 6 5 4 3 2 1

This book is dedicated to everybody who's kind of weird.

A BAD DAY FOR VOODOO

FAQ

Q: Is this book any good?

A: Yeah, I think so. I mean, it's not *The Girl With the Dragon Tattoo* good, but there are worse ways you could spend your time. It's at least better than that one book you read that one time that totally sucked and you were all like "How did this ever get published?" and you shoved it into the garbage disposal and let out a primal roar as you listened to the metal blades grind it up.

Q: Is this book totally realistic?

A: Yes. No matter how silly things get, no matter how weird the characters act, and no matter how far somebody is able to walk with a severely injured foot and not bleed to death, rest assured that every single word in this book is exactly how things would happen in real life. When you find yourself saying, "C'mon, that's so unrealistic!" just remember that you're wrong.

Q: How many people were injured during the writing of this book?

A: We writers are dangerous. Everybody knows that. I'd say that maybe ten or eleven people got slapped around, and one of my assistants injured his back carrying my bags of money. The poor guy had to hold it for almost forty-five minutes while I tried to decide which room should be the "Wow, Look at All of My Money" room. I should have figured that out beforehand. My bad.

Q: Is any material in this book inappropriate for teenagers or those who wish to become teenagers someday?

A: Oh yeah. All of it. Teenagers, don't let any responsible adults catch you reading this, because they will absolutely *freak*. They'll flap their arms around and shout, "This is going to destroy society! Kids copy everything bad they read in books! All is lost, all is lost!"

(*Note to librarians:* I'm only kidding. It's not that bad. I mean, it's gorier than *Winnie the Pooh*, and the word "crap" is used fifteen times, but none of the major curse words are represented, and nobody gets nekkid.)

(*Note to teenagers:* Or DO they…?)

Q: Is this book going to be a series?

A: I don't know. It depends on whether or not everybody dies at the end.

Q: Will this book scare me so badly that I'll wake up screaming from nightmares and need to sleep with the lights on for the next several weeks?

A: Nah.

Q: Does this novel send a positive message to readers?

A: Not really, but this FAQ does. Eat healthy foods. Get plenty of exercise. Study hard. *Don't talk or text during movies.* Sing, even if it's really bad singing. Give somebody you love a hug for no reason, so that they say, "What was that for? What have you done? Do I need to be worried? Tell me!" Don't waste nitroglycerine. *Do. Not. Talk. During. Movies.* (Your grandparents never learned that lesson, but it's not too late for you!)

Q: Anything else?

A: Enjoy the book!

Q: Anything else after that?

A: No, actually I thought the last one was a pretty good stopping point. It ended things on an upbeat note and got you all psyched up to enjoy the novel. Now I'm sort of rambling. Don't worry, I'm not blaming you; I just wish we'd gone right from "Enjoy the book!" into the actual book instead of continuing this FAQ, because I think people are going to start to skim.

Q: Did you?

A: Did I what? I'm not sure what you're asking.

Q: Sorry. I forgot my question. Do you own any pets?

A: I feel like we're drifting off topic here. Let's try to get back to—

Q: Answer the question!

A: Two cats.

Q: How much cottage cheese do you think you could eat in one sitting? Let's say that somebody offered you $1,000 to eat twelve tubs of cottage cheese. Not bathtubs—those plastic tubs that cottage cheese comes in. Could you do it?

A: Enjoy the book!

A BAD DAY FOR VOODOO

CHAPTER 1

"So what if we let the air out of his tires, and then we rig the car so it crushes his arms when he goes to check? He can't give you another F if he doesn't have arms."

"Seems extreme," I said.

"Well…maybe his arms don't actually have to come *off*. We could just make it so they don't work anymore."

Here's the thing about Adam: I knew he was only kidding, but a small part of me suspected that he really would help me rig Mr. Click's car to crush his arms if I asked. Does it make me look bad to admit that my best friend might be a tiny bit psychotic? I hope not.

"I don't want to do anything destructive," I said. "And nothing that could get me suspended. I'll be in enough trouble for the F."

For most of my life, I'd had pretty good luck with my teachers. There were only three of them that I didn't like. Mrs. Teeser, in third grade, was a yeller. She yelled about everything. "Finish your assignment!" "Line up for recess!" "Stop gluing your fingernails together!" My friends and I suspected that she had some sort of medical condition where her head gradually inflated throughout the day, and yelling was the only way to release the pressure. If she didn't yell, her head would pop. We cut her some slack for that.

In seventh grade biology, Mr. Greg was unbelievably strict. He didn't much appreciate jokes that his last name was really a first name, which is understandable, but he treated every moment of every class as if we were discovering a cure for cancer that we could *totally screw up and lose forever* if we lost concentration for a split millisecond. I have to admit that once the school year ended, I stopped disliking him quite so much, but he certainly wasn't one of my favorites.

Most of my other teachers were pretty cool, and I'd go so far as to say that Mrs. Rowell in fifth grade was a genuine life-changing inspiration.

But not Mr. Click.

Mr. Click, who taught my sophomore-year world history class, was just plain *mean*. Not in an ultra-strict "I want you to achieve excellence!" way like Mr. Greg, but in a "Kids suck!" way. I don't think he liked any of us. He didn't even like my girlfriend, Kelley, who got straight A's, always sat up front, and asked intelligent questions, all without being a smarmy, teacher's pet creep.

Maybe if I taught high school history for thirty years, I'd become mean and bitter too. He was a small man, short and thin, with a bushy black mustache and a large haircut-with-a-hole-in-it bald spot. He wore glasses but probably needed a new prescription, because he was always squinting.

Some teachers, when they give you a bad grade, seem like they're mad at you. Sometimes they're disappointed. Sometimes they're a little disgusted. Mr. Click always seemed delighted to hand out a bad grade, and he'd call kids out right in front of everybody. He wouldn't announce, "Hey, Kelley, here's your A-plus!" to the class, but he'd sure say, "Another D, Seth. That doesn't surprise me."

(I'm not Seth. I was just using him as an example.)

I'm Tyler Churchill. My report card was usually pretty good—A's and B's, but they didn't come easy. Except for art, which was a natural talent, I had to study for every test until my butt literally fell off.

(Kelley hated, hated, hated it when people used the word "literally" wrong, so I'll clarify: My butt did not actually detach itself from the rest of my body from the intensity of my studying.)

I wasn't mad at Mr. Click simply because he was pure evil. I was mad because we had a vicious test, the second of five tests that were each worth 10 percent of our grade, and I studied until my eyes figuratively dropped out of my head. And I don't mean that I was a total slacker until the night before and then did a desperate all-night, coffee-fueled cram session. I mean that I studied for that thing for a week. I mean that Kelley said, "Wanna hang out?" and I *said no*. And when she asked if I wanted to study together, I *still said no* because I knew we'd just end up making out.

Do you understand how hard I studied for this test?

I took the test that Friday and nailed it. We walked out of class, and everybody was complaining about how hard it was, especially Adam, but I knew every answer. One hundred percent, baby! Okay, maybe not 100 percent, but at least a 95. I had an awesome weekend.

Monday afternoon, on a cool February morning in Florida, I got my test back. F.

You're probably thinking, "You sure must be dumb to study so hard for a test and still get the answers wrong! Hard to believe you wrote a whole book!"

Nope. He hadn't even marked any of the questions. Just "0/100" and the F at the top.

Kelley turned around in her desk, which was right in front of mine. "What'd you get?"

I folded the test in half. "Ninety-two."

I spent the whole class feeling more than a little sick to my stomach. Our next classes were in the same direction, so normally, Kelley, Adam, and I would walk together, but when the bell rang, I told them to go on ahead. I went up to Mr. Click's desk. "Why'd I get an F?"

He squinted at me. "Cheating."

"Cheating?" What was he talking about? Except for the occasional game of Monopoly, I'd never cheated in my life!

"Your answers were exactly the same as Donnie's, word for word. Do you have another explanation?"

"Yeah, he copied off me!"

"It takes two to cheat. He also received a zero."

"But I didn't *let* him cheat! It's not my fault if he copied my answers! I can't help that!"

"Hmmm."

"This isn't fair."

"Let it be a lesson in personal responsibility."

He really said that. I know, I know, you're outraged on my

behalf, right? I bet you're thinking, "You should've punched that guy in the face!" You can't really punch teachers, though. I mean, you *can*, I suppose, but you really shouldn't. I sure wouldn't.

"I'll retake the test," I said, even though I knew that at least 70 percent of what I'd studied had leaked out of my brain over the weekend. "That'll prove it."

Mr. Click shook his head. "Life and my classroom share a common trait: no second chances."

I stormed out of the room, furious enough to strangle a cute small animal, though the feeling would pass long before I encountered a cute small animal. This was beyond unfair. This was go-to-the-principal unfair. This was "call the local TV station (on a slow news day)" unfair!

I spent all of eighth period economics fuming. And believe me, I can fume.

When school let out, I headed straight to Donnie's locker. Now, I'm not a big guy. I look a bit taller than I really am because of my awesome posture, but my growth spurt was not yet all I hoped it would be, and most other sophomores had a couple of inches on me. Still, I wasn't some scrawny little weakling—I ran track and did well on the swim team—and I did not live in fear of getting beat up or shoved into lockers.

Donnie, on the other hand, was a big guy.

He was not the biggest guy in school. That was a senior named Hank whose flattop haircut emphasized the fact that his head really was kind of flat. But Donnie made the top five, easy, and though I knew we weren't living in a cartoon universe, I did sort of think that he could punch me so hard that my nose would fly off and stick to the wall.

Still, as you'll recall, *I'd passed up the chance to make out with my girlfriend* to study for this thing.

"Hey," I said, walking up to Donnie's locker.

"Hey," he said.

"I got a zero on that test."

He nodded. "Me too."

"It's because you copied off me."

"I didn't copy off you."

"Yes, you did."

"No, I didn't."

"You wrote down all the same answers."

"That's weird."

"So you copied."

"Nope."

"You need to tell Mr. Click."

"Maybe you copied off me."

"I sit in front of you!"

"That's weird."

Then he gave me a look, one that said *You go bye-bye now or Donnie hurt you.*

I left.

I guess I should've been way angrier with Donnie, but Mr. Click had been unpleasant and evil all year, whereas Donnie was like a big, dumb puppy that pees on your video games but doesn't really mean any harm.

Adam and I walked home while I ranted against my unfair

treatment, which is when he said that stuff about squishing Mr. Click's arms with his car. "You definitely need to get revenge," he said.

"Maybe I'll talk to Principal Zelig. There's no way he'll let him get away with this."

"Nah, get revenge first. Egg his windows. TP his house. Leave a dead skunk in his desk drawer. Spread superglue on his chair. Spit in his coffee. Photoshop a picture and post it online. Have twenty or thirty pizzas delivered to his house. Get some laxatives and—"

"Where would I get a dead skunk?"

"I don't know. There's got to be one lying around somewhere."

"I'm just going to talk to Zelig."

"That's weak."

"Sorry."

"Okay, do me a favor. Don't talk to anybody until tomorrow morning. I think I've got an idea. If you're not cool with it, fine, you can tattle to the principal, but I think you'll like it."

"What is it?"

"You'll find out…tomorrow."

"It's not ready yet," Adam told me as we walked to school the next morning. "But Wednesday for sure."

"Can I borrow eighty bucks?" Adam asked on Wednesday morning.

"In what universe do I have an extra eighty bucks?"

"Do you have anything you could sell? A watch or something?"

"Not if you don't tell me what you need it for."

Adam considered that, for a long moment. "Never mind. Friday for sure."

On Friday morning, Adam handed me a wooden box about the size of the Spider-Man lunch box I used to have when I was a little kid. There were weird, curvy symbols on the lid.

"What's this?" I asked.

"Open it."

I opened the lid. Inside was a small doll.

"What's this?" I asked again.

Adam grinned. "It's your very own Mr. Click voodoo doll."

CHAPTER 2

When your best friend gives you a voodoo doll of your history teacher, certain questions come to mind:

1. Are you kidding me?
2. A *voodoo doll*?
3. Seriously?!?
4. Where did you get it?
5. (Two part question) Did you really pay eighty dollars for it, and if so, are you expecting me to pay you back?
6. You don't really believe that voodoo dolls work, do you?
7. How do you use it?
8. How come, even though we've been best friends since the fifth grade, you've never expressed any previous interest in dabbling in this sort of thing, not that I've ever asked if you were into voodoo or anything like that, but still, doesn't it seem like a topic that would have come up sooner?
9. Does anybody else know about this?
10. Are you *insane*?

I started with number 10.

"No," said Adam. "When you think about this, it really makes a lot of sense."

"Wrong. Voodoo is something that seems like a good idea *at the time.*"

"Trust me. This is gonna be awesome."

I picked the doll up out of the box. It was tan-colored and had the texture of a burlap sack. It was mostly featureless—a couple of black dots for eyes and a line across the mouth, but it looked more like a gingerbread man than a representation of Mr. Click.

"It doesn't look anything like him," I said.

"Doesn't matter. It doesn't need to. What's important is that it has his essence."

"If you've spent the past week collecting Mr. Click's essence, our friendship is over."

"Nah, just one strand of hair. Found it right on his desk. No problem at all."

"Where did you get the doll?"

"It's a place called Esmeralda's House of Jewelry. But they have voodoo stuff too. It's across town on Duncan Street, where all of those small shops are."

Duncan Street was where tourists went to be scammed. Not that Geyser, Florida, attracted a lot of tourists. We didn't even have a geyser. The city was named after William Geyser III, who invented some breakthrough in construction in the late 1800s that nobody in Geyser really understands, but that was enough to make him rich and get a city named after him. His statue in our central park was actually built as somebody else in 1913, but that guy turned out to be a bank robber, and the other city sold the statue to us, and everybody agreed to pretend that William Geyser III had worn a beard and gained a few pounds.

Geyser was an okay place to live. We were big enough to support two Walmarts but not big enough that any cool bands ever played here. The city had a bizarre design—we had wealthy, gated communities right next to neighborhoods where you could get knifed for pocket change and a few Tic Tacs. Most of my friends and I lived in the middle-class areas. I sure didn't plan to live here past high school, but I also wasn't looking to pack up my stuff and hitchhike to LA or anything like that.

"I can't believe you went all the way to Duncan Street for that junk."

"This creepy old lady works there. She did all of the enchantment and everything."

"For eighty bucks?"

"Well, yeah, and also a trade." He pulled up his shirtsleeve, revealing a bandage. "A pint of blood. I'm not sure what she's gonna do with it."

I gaped at him. "You gave her *blood*?"

"Why not? My mom donates blood for a Popsicle and a free Thermos. Why not some virgin blood for a discount on a voodoo doll?"

"I can't believe you!" I said, silently vowing that in college I'd find friends who were less deranged. "How could you possibly think this was real?" I asked, shaking the doll.

"Stop that!" he shouted, grabbing the doll away from me.

"You could snap his spine! Look, Tyler, this is serious stuff, and you can't goof around. We're not eleven years old anymore."

At that point, I realized to my slack-jawed, bug-eyed, gasp-inducing amazement that Adam actually believed in the doll. He truly thought that this ridiculous little doll could harm Mr. Click. I'd always known that he wasn't Adam Westell, Boy Genius, but this was far beyond anything I would've expected from him.

"Humor me," he said, carefully placing the doll back in the box and closing the lid. "If it doesn't work, then I'm dumb, and you don't have to pay back the eighty bucks. If it does work...c'mon, imagine how sweet it'll be to jab a pin in that thing right in the middle of class!"

"What'll happen?"

"His leg will hurt. Right in the middle of class!"

"And why exactly is that awesome?"

Adam sighed. "He's standing in front of the class, talking about some war. You poke the doll in the leg. 'Ow! Ow!' Mr. Click gets a sharp pain in his leg! You poke the doll in the arm. 'Ow! Ow!' Sharp pain in the arm! He'll be freaking out! Poke him all over the place. He won't know if he's having a heart attack or his appendix is going to burst or if he caught an STD."

"And that's hilarious?"

"Do I really need to explain why having Mr. Click feel pain is a good thing? The guy is Satan in a blender with Hitler!"

"You know you wasted your money, right? It's the most wasted eighty bucks you'll ever spend."

"I did it for you."

"Well, in the future, don't do things like that for me. Figure out other things to do. Buy me a gift card. C'mon, Adam, voodoo dolls aren't real! What's the matter with you?"

Adam traced his index finger along one of the symbols on the box lid. "I'm not saying that I completely believe it, but you should've talked to that old lady at the shop. She was really convincing. The way I look at it, even if the doll turns out to be a complete rip-off—"

"Not if. When."

"—*if* the doll turns out to be fake, it'll still make you feel better to jab pins into it during class, right? Like when you put somebody's picture on a dartboard? That always feels good."

"I'm not doing it."

"I went to a lot of trouble to figure out a way for you to get even with Mr. Satan Hitler. You're not even going to humor me? How is your life worse if you poke pins in a doll?"

I supposed Adam had a point. This was really stupid, but it wasn't like he was asking me to run naked through a pep rally. (He had in the past, and I had declined.) Ultimately, sticking a pin into a doll was not a big deal.

"Why don't you do it?" I asked.

"I'm not the one who got screwed. I deserved my F. This is about you."

"All right. Fine. Whatever. How does it work?"

Adam grinned. "Exactly the way you'd expect a voodoo doll to work." He removed the box lid and picked up a pin from inside. "You stick the pin into the doll, and Mr. Click feels it. Take it out, and the pain goes away."

"Does it have to be that pin?"

"Nah. The old lady just threw in a couple of them for free."

"Have you tested it?"

Adam shook his head. "It's no fun if you can't see his reaction. Do it today in class. Don't tell Kelley."

That wasn't going to be a problem. Kelley kind of liked Adam, dubbing him "quirky," but if I told her that I was thinking about playing along with a voodoo-doll scheme, she would've instantly broken up with me. She was very practical about those sorts of things. "Dabbling in the nonexistent supernatural realm? New boyfriend, please."

When we got to school, I put the box in my locker and went to algebra class. I didn't think about the doll much during the day because, as I've said before, it was stupid. Between sixth and seventh period, I went to my locker, took the doll out of the box, and put it in my backpack.

I wished that I could just lie about it ("Pinned it. Nothin'."), but Adam sat right next to me.

Is it possible that maybe, just maybe, a small part of me believed that the doll was truly enchanted with the magical power of voodoo? Was there some insignificant part of my psyche that wanted vengeance with such intensity that I subconsciously convinced myself that this could work?

Nope. The doll was a bunch of crap.

When I sat at my desk, I left my backpack unzipped on the floor next to me. I wasn't going to actually take the doll out, because voodoo or not, I sure didn't want anybody to see me holding a doll in history class.

The bell rang, and Mr. Click gave us his traditional afternoon scowl. "Did everybody read pages two-forty through two-fifty-three like you were supposed to?"

Most of the kids nodded.

"Good. Then this pop quiz should pose no problem."

The class groaned. Mr. Click handed a stack of papers to the first kid in each row so they could pass them back. I had a sudden desire to poke a voodoo doll right between the eyes, but I definitely didn't want him to see me reaching into my backpack before a quiz.

The quiz sucked.

After ten minutes, Mr. Click told us that our time was up and to pass the quizzes forward. As we did so, Mr. Click stared right at me, and his beady eyes seemed to say, "I know you have a voodoo doll in your backpack, and if you try to stick a pin in it, I will destroy you and everyone you've ever loved."

A moment later I decided that his eyes probably weren't saying that. It was more likely "Cheating is bad."

Mr. Click collected the quizzes, set them on his desk, and then began the lecture. It's worth noting that he was not an engaging speaker. He tended to ramble and repeat himself and drain every possible bit of potential interest from the subject matter. Though I was no history buff, *some* of this stuff was kind of cool...but not when the words came from Mr. Click's mouth.

To get the basic gist of what I'm talking about, pick any paragraph from this book and read it out loud in a monotone. Reread it over and over and over and over until you want to bash your head against a hard surface over and over and over and over so that your brain can escape and flee for sanctuary. That's what his lectures were like.

About half an hour into the class, when Mr. Click had his back turned because he was scrawling something onto the chalkboard, Adam reached over and poked me in the shoulder. He glared at me and mouthed, "Do it."

Fine. I'd do it.

Mr. Click turned back toward us and continued his agonizing lecture. It was about four or five minutes later (felt like sixty or seventy) before he returned his attention to the chalkboard.

I casually leaned down and reached into my backpack. It shuffled a bit, but the nice thing about having a straight-A student for a girlfriend is that she was paying too close attention to what the teacher was saying to turn around and see what her idiot boyfriend was doing right behind her.

The pins were in a small pouch that I'd purposely left unzipped. I quickly picked up one of them.

I poked it deep into the doll's left leg.

Mr. Click let out a shriek of pain that ripped through my eardrums.

And then his leg shot off from his body in a spray of blood and bone as if it had been fired from a cannon.

The leg slid across the tile floor, leaving a thick red trail and stopped only when it struck the wall.

I guess it goes without saying that everybody in the classroom began to figuratively scream their heads off.

CHAPTER 3

Kelley was the first one up. Mr. Click lay on the floor, bellowing and clutching his stump, while I thought, *Oh my God, oh my God, oh my God, oh my God…*

Kids were sobbing and screaming and panicking, and there were at least two confirmed vomiters. There was blood everywhere. I couldn't breathe.

I plucked the pin out of the doll. Sadly, Mr. Click's leg did not slide back and reattach itself.

What had I done?

What kind of horrible monster was I?

What the hell kind of steroid-enhanced voodoo doll was this?

"Get me a ruler!" Kelley shouted, obviously thinking, *tourniquet.* There was blood on her glasses, but none had yet spurted onto her blonde hair, which was pulled back into a ponytail.

I stood up, feeling dizzy. A few kids had their cell phones out and were frantically dialing. Two girls, Helen and Andrea, ran out of the classroom to get help.

Adam was frozen in his seat, looking positively horrified. Which was a relief—that was much better than seeing him sitting there, rubbing his hands together, and cackling in malicious glee.

I stumbled up to the front of the room, pausing for a moment as my vision blurred. Then I crouched down next to Kelley and Mr. Click. Kelley was clearly freaked out yet was staying composed. Somebody handed her a ruler.

"Give me your shirt," she said to me.

I stripped off my shirt and gave it to her. She wrapped it around the ruler and Mr. Click's stump, then began to twist the ruler.

I don't have a solid memory of the next few minutes. I know that Mr. Jenkins, who taught economics next door, came in to see what all of the commotion was about. He didn't think we were overreacting. Then the principal, a couple more teachers, and finally some cops and two paramedics arrived.

They got Mr. Click onto a gurney and wheeled my screaming history teacher out of the classroom. Yes, one of the paramedics brought his leg with them.

After they left, I gave Kelley a hug, and she totally lost it, sobbing against my bare chest.

Our three-month anniversary was tomorrow. Apparently, my present to her was a ghastly, horrific experience that would forever haunt her. She'd probably give me a book.

This went way beyond any thirst for revenge I might have had. Even if I'd believed that the doll would work, which I've already clearly established that I most certainly did not, I didn't expect any reaction stronger than "Ow!" Maybe a "Dammit!" If I could have gotten an "Ow!" and a "Dammit!" out of him, I would have felt avenged enough.

Obviously there were certain questions that I wanted to ask of my good buddy Adam. I supposed that they should wait. Pointing at him and shouting, "*What did you make me dooooo?!?*" would be a bad idea until such a time as there weren't twenty-eight kids, three teachers, and a principal in the room.

Everybody in class was quickly questioned by the police, who were quite understandably confused as to how such a thing could happen. I'm not sure how my fellow history students reported the afternoon's events, but I assumed that they were all variations on "He was talking about World War I, and then suddenly, *his leg flew off.*"

Did I need to be nervous? Somebody might have seen me reach into my backpack seconds before the incident, but so what? What could I have had in my backpack that made somebody's leg shoot off? A detonator? How could I strap explosives to Mr. Click's upper left leg without him being aware of it? There hadn't been an actual *bang*, and if explosives were involved, there'd be burn marks on his leg, so the police would quickly rule that out, which meant that the only possible connection between me reaching into my backpack and his leg coming off could be "voodoo doll," and I didn't think they'd go there.

When it was my turn to give a statement, the cop was reasonably polite and even had somebody find me a new shirt to wear. Though I babbled a bit (Okay, a lot...Okay, more than a lot), under these circumstances, I don't think it seemed suspicious.

By the time we were allowed to leave, the press had surrounded the school. Kelley, Adam, and I gave a quick "No comment!" and got into the back of Kelley's mother's car. Other kids were enthusiastically talking to reporters about what had happened, but we just wanted to get out of there as quickly as possible. The doll was still in my backpack, but though I'd put it back inside its box, every bump on the road sent a jolt through my heart. I was glad I wasn't the one driving; it's hard enough to keep your hands at ten and two without worrying that you're going to jostle a voodoo doll and kill your teacher.

Kelley's mom had always been nice to me in an I-know-my-daughter-can-do-better-but-I-suppose-she-could-also-do-a-whole-lot-worse manner, and she seemed genuinely concerned about my mental health as we pulled up in front of my home. I assured her that I'd be fine, and Adam assured her that he didn't need to be dropped off at his own house.

I gave Kelley the kind of kiss you give your girlfriend when she's been through a traumatic experience and her mom is right there, and they drove off.

Finally, Adam and I were alone.

"So," I said, keeping my voice as calm as possible, "is it safe to say that you thought something *else* was going to happen?"

"I had no idea!" Adam insisted. "Not a clue! Did you see that? Did you see it? I—I—I—I didn't think legs could do that! Oh my God! That was insane! Did you see it?"

"Why did it do that?"

"I don't know! I don't know! I don't know!"

"They didn't give you any kind of warning?"

"No! It was only supposed to sting! I swear to you what happened wasn't the plan!" Adam closed his eyes and took several deep breaths.

"What if he dies?"

Adam opened his eyes. "He won't, will he? People don't die from losing legs, not if the ambulance gets there right away, do they?"

"Did you see how much blood he lost?"

"Yes! It was all over the place! That was, like, ten times as much blood as I thought somebody would lose if their leg got cut off. Oh my God!" He was almost crying now. "Do you think they'll find out we did it?"

"I don't know. I mean, if you think about it, I don't see how they could. A CSI team isn't going to expose a voodoo curse, are they? We just need to get rid of this doll!"

Adam brightened. "We'll burn it!"

"No, we won't freaking burn it!"

"Oh yeah, right, right, right. Terrible idea."

"Can the old lady…you know, deactivate it?"

"I don't know. I didn't ask. She'd have to be able to, right?"

"Maybe that's something you should have researched before you bought a voodoo doll!"

"You're the one who stuck the pin in it!"

I did not punch him. Praise me for my restraint.

"Don't hit me," he said, noticing my clenched fist. "I'm sorry. It was all my fault!"

"Yes."

"I'll make it right. I'll fix it, I promise."

"How can you possibly fix it?"

"I mean I'll fix the doll. The surgeons will fix Mr. Click. They've got his leg with them—they'll just use lasers to put it back on. He'll be okay. He never wears shorts. Should I call the old lady?"

I shook my head. "If this does come back to us, we don't want any record of any calls to a voodoo shop."

"Yeah, yeah, good thinking. I'll take it back tonight. We'll be fine. Leg lasered back on, doll deactivated…everything will be awesome." He reached for my backpack. "Give me the doll."

Put yourself in my position. Your friend, who is looking crazy-eyed and a little scary, wants you to give him a doll with unspeakable powers. This particular friend has demonstrated on numerous occasions that he is prone to very poor judgment. He's a good pal, and you like hanging out with him; yet you also suspect that if he is left responsible for the doll, he might drop it, lose it, or somehow accidentally cause your history teacher to become a four-limb amputee.

So you tell him, "I'll hang onto it."

Adam's eyes turned crazier and scarier. "Are you going to hand it over to the cops?"

"No!"

"You're going to turn me in, aren't you?"

"No! That would be like turning myself in! What's the matter with you?"

"Why won't you give me the doll?"

"We'll take it there together!"

"*Give me the doll!*"

Adam lunged at me, knocking me to the ground. I got the eagerly awaited opportunity to punch him, though there was no joy or satisfaction in the act, just a hurt fist. Adam, who didn't get punched very often, howled in pain and crawled off me, hand against his jaw.

"I'm sorry," he said.

"What's the matter with you?"

"I'm flipping out, okay? I admit it! My brain is weak."

"Well, stop it! You could have wrecked the doll even more! We have nothing to worry about, as long as we don't act like complete morons!" I picked up my backpack and stood back up.

"Can I please have the doll?"

"No."

"I'd really like the doll."

"We're taking it back together, all right? My mom will get home before yours, so when she does, we'll borrow the car and take the doll back to the voodoo shop."

"What do we do until then? Twitch?"

"Let's see what they're saying on TV."

We went inside my house, plopped down on the living room couch, and after the usual five-minute hunt for the remote control, I turned on the television.

"—and a strange story becomes even stranger," said the reporter, standing outside of the hospital, as a caption let us know that this was LIVE. "Mr. Ronald Click, a high school teacher who severed his left leg in a bizarre accident during class, has been pronounced dead."

"*No!*" Adam shouted.

"We don't have all the details, but he reportedly died on the operating table about five minutes ago…from a broken neck."

We stared at the television screen for a very long time. The reporter gave more details, and I'm pretty sure Adam said a lot of things, but quite honestly, I didn't hear any of it.

"I think we killed him," I finally said.

"Maybe not," said Adam. "Maybe...maybe the doctors dropped him."

I've never seen a truly insane person, the kind you have to lock in a padded cell, but I thought they probably looked a lot like Adam did at that moment. I honestly didn't know if he was going to start sobbing or drop to the floor and cackle with maniacal laughter.

I opened my backpack, took out the box, and removed the lid.

The doll's neck was bent backward.

If this weren't a true story, I'd make up something clever I had said. Something like "Well, this rules out the doctor-drop theory!" but more clever than that. But since this is entirely true, I just stared at it with my mouth hanging open, thinking that now might be a pretty good time for a heart attack.

"You killed him," Adam said.

"*I* killed him?"

"You had the doll!"

"It should have been in a better box!"

"Don't blame the box!"

"Why wasn't it padded?"

"I don't know!"

"You attacked me!" I shouted. "If it's anybody's fault, it's—"

Adam lunged for the doll, but I shoved him to the floor. He got up quickly, raised his fists, seemed to think better of the idea, and lowered them.

"I'm not gonna let you turn me in," he said.

"I wasn't going to!"

"I'll make sure it doesn't happen!" Adam turned and ran out of my living room. I heard the door slam as he left the house. I thought about going after him, but no, I needed to let him blow off some steam and calm himself down.

I paced around for a few moments and then decided that I needed the help of somebody much smarter than me. I took out my cell phone to call Kelley.

CHAPTER 4

I had seventeen text messages from sixteen different people. Some samples:

OMG Click is dead!!!!!!!!

Did u hear about Mr. Click? Funny but sad!

Was it ur class when his leg popped off? Did u see it?
I heard it was the grossest thing ever!

Click = dead. Me = :)

Check Google! Mr. Click is DEAD! I never thought I
would be sad but I'm crying right now!

I closed out of my text messages and touched Kelley's name to call her. Then I quickly touched End to disconnect the call. I needed to think about what I was going to say. I couldn't just blurt out "AAAAHHH!!! I killed him! I killed him! Ahh! Ahh!

Ahh!" I desperately needed her advice, but I had to be cool about the way I asked for it.

Was calling her a bad idea?

Maybe. She was one more person who'd know what I'd done.

But we needed a non-dumb person involved. Left on our own, Adam and I would just bumble our way right into prison. Kelley could help us find the elements of the situation that we'd overlooked, the things that might lead the cops right to my front door.

"*Freeze!*" they'd shout after kicking the door down. "*Drop the voodoo doll!*"

"*Never!*" I'd scream. "*If you coppers want the doll, you'll have to—*"

Ratatatatatatatatatatatatatatatatatat!!!

"*Ugh!*" I'd say as 387 bullets pounded into my chest. Then I'd drop the doll like they'd asked.

Yep, that was exactly what would happen if I didn't get Kelley's advice. I called her again.

"How're you doing?" she asked, answering on the first ring.

"Did you hear?"

"Hear what?"

"Mr. Click died."

There was a long moment of silence.

"Still there?" I asked.

"Yeah, I'm still…that's so awful…"

"That's insane, isn't it?"

"So he bled to death?"

I wondered if I should gently ease her into the whole broken-neck concept. "I'm not sure," I said. "All I know is that he died."

It occurred to me that if I was calling my girlfriend to confess my role in the tragedy and beg for advice, I probably shouldn't start lying fifteen seconds into the conversation.

Kelley sniffled. "I don't even know what to say."

"What if this was my fault?" I asked.

"Excuse me?"

"What if I was responsible for Mr. Click's death?"

"What are you saying? Is this guilt because you don't think you did enough to help him?"

"You don't think I did enough to help him?"

"Tyler..."

"I gave you my shirt!"

"Tyler!"

"Okay, okay, I'm sorry. Hear me out. You're good at science. Can you think of any possible scientific explanation for what happened?"

"I don't know."

"You can't, can you? Nothing like that ever happens. There may be records of things like spontaneous combustion, but there aren't any known cases where somebody's leg just popped off! I guess there's leprosy, but even if he was a leper, his leg wouldn't fly across the room, right?"

"Spontaneous combustion doesn't exist."

"Good, so this helps prove my point. There's no rational explanation for this."

"There's always a rational explanation."

"Like what?"

Kelley was silent for a few seconds. "Like he'd already lost his leg and didn't tell anybody about it. He was giving the lecture and he turned too quickly, so the stitches popped, and he panicked and kicked his leg across the room."

"That's..." I started to say *crazy*, but it actually wasn't such a bad explanation. Maybe that was it! Maybe he *had* already lost his leg, perhaps as the result of clumsy chain saw handling, and he went to some discount doctor who used cheap thread, and the voodoo doll had nothing to do with—

Okay, that was a stretch, so I finished my sentence, "...crazy."

"Well, what do *you* think happened?"

I tried to figure out how best to bring up the subject. "Do you believe in voodoo dolls?" Nice transition. Smooth.

"Do you *think* I believe in voodoo dolls?"

"No."

"Good."

"But let's pretend that you do."

"Let's not."

"Just for pretend."

"Tyler, I'm not in the mood for games. Tell me what you're trying to say, or I'm hanging up."

"Adam bought me a voodoo doll of Mr. Click, and today in class, I jabbed a pin in its leg, and Mr. Click's real leg shot off, and we got into a fight, and we dropped the doll, and its neck broke, and then I saw on the news that Mr. Click died from a broken neck."

Kelley did not immediately respond.

"Are you still—"

"Can I call you back?" she asked.

"Sure."

She hung up. I stood there, staring at the phone in my hand, wondering if I'd made a terrible, terrible mistake.

I'd gotten seven more text messages during our conversation. They were all variations on the "OMG!" theme.

I felt sick to my stomach. Did I have time for a quick puke break before Kelley called me back?

Was she calling the cops?

What was Adam doing right now? Was *he* calling the cops?

Did I have anything I could hurriedly make into a bullet-proof vest?

My phone vibrated in my hand, and I yelped and dropped it. I picked it up, thankful that nobody had heard the yelp or seen the drop. It was Kelley.

"Hey," I said.

"He *did* die of a broken neck!"

"I know."

"How is that possible?"

"Voodoo sucks."

"Tell me exactly what happened."

I told her pretty much everything I've written here so far, in not quite as much detail and without as many side comments. She only interrupted me four times, to say "Are you kidding me?" twice, "Are you serious?" once, and one combo platter of "You can't be serious! Are you kidding me?"

When the story lapped itself (I left out the part where I called her, figuring it was unnecessary), Kelley took a moment to process everything I'd told her and then said, "If this is a joke, I will kill you."

"It's not."

"I'll kill you and then break up with your corpse."

"It's not a joke."

"I mean it. You think I won't really kill you, but I will. If you're playing around, I will stab you and stab you and stab you."

"Got it."

"Okay, I won't kill you, but I'll break up with you. Immediately. The second I hear that you're joking, you no longer have a girl-friend, and I will make sure that you *never* have a girlfriend. I can make that happen. I've got connections. Our teacher is dead. It's not material for a prank."

I tried not to yell, "*I said this wasn't a freakin' joke!*" If our roles were reversed, I would've required just as many reassurances that she wasn't messing with me. That said, I was starting to get annoyed at the time we were wasting when we could be strategizing.

"Not a joke," I said.

She let out a deep sigh. "Okay, we'll pretend I believe you. Where's Adam?"

"I'm not sure."

"Don't you think that's something you should know?"

"Yes," I admitted.

"Call him. Keep calling until he answers. I'll be right over."

CHAPTER 5

Adam's phone rang five times and then went to voice mail.

"Hi," said Adam on his message. "I'm not available to take your call right now…or *am* I? Maybe if you wait, I'll answer. Wait…wait…wait for it…could be any second now…keep waiting…I hope you didn't have other plans…wait…might be getting closer…wait for it…no, I guess I'm not answering. Leave a message at the musical note."

It was pretty clear why Adam's pool of friends was so small.

Beep.

"Adam, I need you to call me back! We have to talk about this!" Should I tell him that I'd involved Kelley without his permission? Nah, probably not. "If we stay calm, we can figure this out. Call me."

I ended the call, called him back, and listened to his voice mail message again. "Seriously, dude, call me back," I said.

I called him again. "Just in case you're only checking every third message, call me back."

Okay, that was sufficient. Hopefully, he wasn't purposely ignoring my calls.

I couldn't think of anything else productive to do, so I paced around my room some more.

Did Mr. Click have a family? I'd never really thought about that before. I'd always assumed that he went home in the evening and sat alone in his house, snarling, but maybe there were those who loved him, who were devastated that he was gone. How many people were heartbroken because of what I'd done?

Suddenly I wanted to cry.

I was pretty sure he didn't have a wife and kids, but were his parents still alive? Did he have brothers and sisters? Aunts? Uncles? A dog? Hamsters?

This wasn't my fault. I hadn't known what was going to happen. All I'd wanted was for his leg to hurt a little bit. No, I hadn't even wanted that. I was only humoring Adam. I wasn't the bad guy. I wasn't some kind of ghastly, bloodthirsty, teacher-murdering monster.

I still felt horrible.

A few minutes later, a car pulled into my driveway, and I met Kelley at the door. Her eyes were puffy, and she wiped her nose with a tissue as we sat down on the couch in my living room. I had the box with the doll on my lap.

"For now, we'll pretend that I believe you," she said.

"Do you?"

"No. I don't think you're purposely lying, but I'm not ready to believe in voodoo dolls quite yet. Show it to me."

I opened the lid.

"It doesn't look anything like him," she said.

"I guess it doesn't need to."

"So you broke its neck?"

"Yeah."

"Then the damage is done, right? As far as the doll is concerned, there's nothing else that can happen."

"Well…I mean…I'm not sure. I guess that if more stuff happened to the doll, more stuff would happen to Mr. Click's body. His corpse could just start mangling itself on the autopsy table."

"Okay, so—again, pretending that I believe in the doll—there *is* more stuff that can go wrong. A self-mutilating cadaver will raise too many questions. We have to make sure that absolutely nothing else happens to the doll. Bury it."

"Bury it? Do you think that could…I don't know, bury his soul or something?"

"Bury his soul?"

"I'm not sure what I meant by that," I admitted.

"By that line of thinking, you carried his soul around in your backpack all day. His soul is fine. You could buy a safe, but then your parents would want to know why you have a safe in your room. I guess hiding the doll under your bed might be good enough. We only need to protect it for a few days; once he's buried or cremated, it won't matter." She frowned. "You know what? If we bury him, a dog might dig him up. We don't want a bite to come out of his arm in front of the mortician."

"Definitely not."

"So we hide the doll under your bed. If for some bizarre reason the police search your house, the most they'll find is a doll that doesn't look anything like Mr. Click. On to Adam: What do you think he's doing?"

I shrugged. "I have no idea."

"Think like Adam."

"That's too scary."

"I'm serious, Tyler. You can pretty much get out of this mess by doing nothing. It won't help your conscience, but as far as avoiding going to prison, all you have to do is not screw things up worse. Do you think Adam could be doing something at this very moment that's screwing things up worse?"

Aw, crap.

"Yes!" I said. "Of course he could. He could be ruining everything. I don't even want to think about how much damage he could be doing. Crap!"

"And you've called?"

"Yes."

"And left messages?"

"Yes."

"Messages that could get you in trouble if somebody besides Adam heard them?"

Damn! A trick question! I thought for a split second, then answered honestly, "No, I only said we needed to talk."

"Did you text him?"

"No. He's scared of texts."

"What?"

"It's a long story."

"How did I not know that?"

"I thought I mentioned it that one time."

"No, that's something I would have remembered. How can you be scared of texts?"

"Right before his grandfather died, he looked up at Adam, took his hand, and said...You know what, we're getting distracted."

Kelley nodded. "Yeah, sorry. Maybe you should lie to him."

"Like how?"

"Tell him that if he comes back, you'll give him the doll. But don't say 'doll' on the voice mail. Be vague."

"What happens when he comes back?"

"You don't give him the doll."

I called Adam again. At the tone, I said, "Adam, it's me. I really need to talk to you. I'll give it back to you, okay? We can work this out." I hung up, secretly proud of myself for not messing up and saying "doll." You've got to savor the small victories. I looked at Kelley. "So now what?"

"TV?"

"Sure."

And so, after shoving the box with the doll in it under my bed, Kelley and I watched TV. I really, really, really hope you don't think of me as a role model, but if you do, you may be disappointed to learn that instead of taking further action to solve my problem, I watched some episodes of *South Park* that I'd seen a few times already. I apologize for letting you down, but if even Kelley thought there was nothing more we could do, I certainly wasn't going to be the one to shout, "Eureka!"

Adam didn't call me back.

My mom came home around six and asked how my day went.

I told her, leaving out the voodoo but leaving in Mr. Click's leg and death.

Of the next six minutes, one minute and fifty-two seconds were spent convincing her that I wasn't playing some mean-spirited joke, forty-eight seconds were spent being hugged while she cried, two minutes and one second were spent explaining why I didn't immediately call her (official answer: I was handling it fine, no really, I was fine, seriously, I was fine, I didn't want to disturb her at work, I was fine, really, I was fine), and one minute and nineteen seconds were spent insisting that, yes, I did love her, and if anything like this ever happened again, I would call her so she could mother me.

Then she started on Kelley. This lasted only three minutes and twenty seconds.

Admittedly, I felt pretty bad about this. Despite my preoccupation with the voodoo situation, I should have called my mom and dad. That said, my guilt over causing the death of a human being was a *little* more intense, so my mom-guilt would have to stay shoved near the back of my brain for the time being.

My dad came home shortly after that, though he was more interested in the technical aspects of how a teacher's leg could just pop off than my fragile emotional state.

My cell phone rang. Adam. Finally!

"Hey," I said. "How's it going?"

"Meet me in Trollen Park in fifteen minutes," he said, speaking slowly and carefully. I think he was trying to sound like a supervillain. Then he hung up.

"Yeah, sure, no problem," I said, speaking into the dead line.

"Let me ask my parents." I lowered the phone. "Is it okay if I give Adam a quick ride? He forgot to get a birthday card for his mom."

Had I thought about this for an extra half second, I would have picked an excuse that couldn't be verified as a lie with a quick visit to Facebook. (For example, "He needed a ride to the post office" would have worked just as well.) But it was too late now.

"Of course," my mom said.

"Thanks." I pretended to hang up and slipped the phone back into my pocket.

Adam hadn't said to bring the doll. Should I bring it? Leave it at home? "Bring the doll" might have been implied, but he didn't actually *say* it, so I decided to leave the doll safely under my bed.

Fifteen minutes later, with Kelley in the passenger seat, I parked my mom's car outside of Trollen Park, a small playground where I spent long hours as a little kid, though pretty much nobody ever went there anymore. Adam was seated on the bottom of the slide. Another symbol-covered box rested on his lap.

CHAPTER 6

"Uh, hi," I said as we walked toward the slide.

Adam glared at Kelley. "What's she doing here?"

"She knows about the doll, but it's okay, because she doesn't believe us. What's in the box?"

"Wouldn't you like to know?"

"Yes. Very much."

"Come closer."

"Okay, Adam, you're totally creeping me out," I said. "I understand why you're mad, but that doesn't mean you have to turn evil."

"I'm not evil."

"Well, you're acting kind of evil. Please stop."

"That's close enough," said Adam when Kelley and I were about ten feet away. He gave us a smile that was a combination of *Oh yeah, dude, I'm totally evil* and *I want my mommy.*

He lifted the lid off the box.

Inside was something shocking, something horrifying, something that filled my heart with absolute dread, something that...okay, you've already guessed that it was another voodoo doll, right? I don't want to insult your intelligence by

JEFF STRAND

trying to stretch out the suspense too much if you're ahead of the story.

Yeah, it was a voodoo doll. It looked almost exactly like the first one: tan-colored, the texture of a burlap sack, mostly feature-less, etc. I gasped. Every sweat gland on my body activated at the same time. My vision blurred a bit. My stomach flopped around. But I did not wet myself.

"You have *got* to be kidding me," said Kelley.

"I've never been more serious in my life," said Adam, who did look pretty darn serious.

"So…what's that for?" I asked.

"Don't you know?"

I shook my head. "If Mr. Click is already dead, why would you need another voodoo doll of him?"

Don't worry, I'm not *that* dumb. I was merely trying to throw Adam off balance by saying something idiotic. I'm not sure whether my ruse fooled him or not. Adam lifted the doll out of the box. "Does he look familiar?"

"What are you going to do with it?"

"I'm sorry," said Kelley. "I'm used to being the one who knows what's going on, and I have no idea what's happening here. Who is that doll supposed to be?"

"Me," I said.

Kelley scowled. "Adam, what on earth is the matter with you? Our teacher is dead, and you're still going to play these stupid games? Seriously, I feel like I should just punch you right in the face."

"Please don't threaten him," I said in a much higher pitch of voice than I'd intended.

"Do you need a demonstration?" Adam asked.

"*No! No! No demonstration!*" I requested.

"I mean it," Kelley told him. "I will kick your scrawny twig butt into the ground. I've never been in a fight in my life, but I will destroy you."

Adam curled his index finger and then flicked the doll in the stomach.

During my sixteen years on this planet, I've been fortunate enough to never have been punched in the gut with full force by a heavyweight boxer. But I'm pretty sure it felt exactly like Adam flicking the doll. I let out the loudest "Ooomph!" in human history, doubled over, lost my balance, and fell to the ground.

Kelley crouched down next to me. "Are you guys playing a…?" She trailed off, because she could tell that I wasn't faking. My face was probably bright red. I'm sure that a fine, classically trained actor could mimic the blow to the stomach and make it convincing, but Kelley knew that I was a lousy actor who had only gotten into one school play, and only because not enough guys tried out.

I coughed and lay on the ground and clutched at my stomach and hoped that Kelley would make good on her promise to destroy Adam. I said a whole bunch of words that probably wouldn't offend you but which I will leave out of the story anyway.

When I could speak without oodles of profanity again, I said, "So what do you want?"

"I want you to know that I've got a voodoo doll of you, and if you go to the police, I'll jab it with a pin!"

"I was never gonna go to the police!"

"Well, now I *know* you won't!"

"You knew it already!"

"Not one hundred percent!"

"What do you mean not one hundred percent? What possible reason could I have ever had to run to the cops?"

"You...you...you...you...you could've gone insane." Adam frowned. "Uh, sort of like me. Sorry."

I was positively furious. "Things were going just fine," I said. "I mean, not so much the dead Mr. Click thing, but it would've all blown over! We didn't have to do anything except not panic! And now you've put my life and leg in danger to keep me from doing something I was never going to do anyway!"

Adam looked as if he couldn't decide whether to yell back or apologize again. His lower lip began to tremble.

"You'd better not be about to cry," I said.

His shoulders began to quiver.

"I'm serious. I don't want to see that crap," I said.

His face scrunched up a bit.

"Don't do it," I said.

Adam cried.

So, yeah, on top of all of the other stuff he'd done, Adam had to go and create an awkward moment for everybody. Kelley and I just stood there, exchanging uncomfortable glances while we watched him cry. I certainly wasn't going to give him a comforting hug.

A car drove by, and I immediately thought, "Oh no, they're going to see Adam crying and realize that we accidentally killed our history teacher with a voodoo doll!" but the thought was fleeting.

"Are you done?" I asked Adam as he wiped his nose off on his sleeve.

"Gimme another ten seconds."

He cried for another ten seconds, then sniffled and looked at me. I think his expression was supposed to melt my heart, but it did not.

"So now what?" he asked.

We both looked at Kelley.

Kelley sighed. "You know, Tyler, I'm putting up with a lot for a relationship that was never going to last past high school."

"I know."

"Okay. So. Hmm. I guess we could get a safety deposit box or rent a storage unit or something to keep the doll protected. But then you have to spend the rest of your life hoping that the bank won't get hit by a hurricane. Are you comfortable with that?"

"Not really."

Kelley turned to Adam. "Where did you get the doll?"

"It's this place called Esmeralda's House of Jewelry."

"On Duncan Street," I told her. "Where all those little shops are."

"So, what? Half an hour away?"

"About that."

"Then we take the doll back. If they can give it power, they can take it away."

"Are you sure?" I asked.

"Two minutes ago, I didn't believe in voodoo, so no."

"How did you even get the doll if you were out of money?" I asked Adam. "And how did you get my essence?"

"Save the info dump," said Kelley, taking out her cell phone. "I'm going to find their number on Google. Adam, is there anything else you can tell us that might help?"

"That I'm really sorry?"

"Ask me how much that helped. Go on, ask me, jackass."

"I'm sorry. I really am. But, you know, it's like what Anthony Hopkins said in *Psycho*: 'We all go a little crazy sometimes.'"

"That was Anthony Perkins," I said.

"No, it was Anthony Hop...oh, dammit! I can't do *anything* right today!"

"If you cry again, I'll break your nose."

"That's not cool."

"Shhh." Kelley tapped the screen a few times and then held her phone to her ear. We all stood there silently for a few moments, and then she disconnected the call. "I got their voice mail. They're open until seven. If we leave now, we can make it."

"Awesome!" I felt an incredible sense of relief. They had to be able to take away the doll's curse, right? Nobody would just hand a deadly doll to an idiot without some way to fix things.

Everything would be okay. I would not have my own rocket-leg experience.

"How about you give me the doll?" I asked Adam.

He nodded and handed it to me. I held the doll carefully, the way you hold a baby that would explode if you dropped it.

"Did you do any other horrible things we should know about?" Kelley asked him.

Adam shook his head.

"Are you sure? Now's the time to spill everything."

"Nothing. I mean, I started to write a letter that would go out to the media if I turned up dead, but I didn't get very far."

I stopped walking and gaped at him. "Are you kidding me?"

"Don't look at me like that! I didn't know what you were gonna do!"

"Unbelievable." I resumed walking while I took out my cell phone and called my mom.

"Tyler?" she answered.

"Hey, Mom, Adam can't find what he needs, so we're going to keep looking. I just wanted to let you know."

"No, you need to come home. You've had a traumatic experience."

"I should only be about another hour."

"Seriously, Tyler, come home. I mean it."

"I'll be quick."

"Tyler, come home. That's an order."

"Uh, okay. I'm on my way," I lied, and then I hung up. Something fun to deal with later, I supposed.

We got in the car, Kelley in the front seat and Adam in the back. I held the doll out toward Kelley. "Could you hold this? Carefully?"

"No." She shook her head. "No way."

"If I let Adam hold it, it'll be a pretzel."

"I'm not taking responsibility for that thing. If you brake too fast, I could crush your head."

"I trust you."

"I'm glad you trust me, but I don't want to be riding in a car with a driver who has a crushed head."

"Fair enough."

"I'll hold it," Adam offered.

"Nah."

Kelley didn't have her driver's license yet, and to be completely honest, I wouldn't have trusted myself to hold the doll even if she did.

"Give me the box," I told Adam as I pulled the lever to pop open the trunk. He leaned forward and handed it to me, and I carefully placed the doll inside. Then I got back out of the car, set the box inside the trunk, pushed some blankets up against it for additional padding, said a silent prayer, and then shut the lid of the trunk.

I'd be totally fine. The doll would be safe until we could un-voodoo it.

As I started the engine, Kelley entered the address into the GPS. We'd get there at 6:51. Cutting it close, yeah, but I was pretty good at trimming a few minutes off the GPS's projected arrival time.

We drove away from the park. I certainly don't want to ruin this story for you, but I don't think it's too big of a spoiler to say that things were not totally fine.

CHAPTER 7

"Are we lost?" Adam asked.

"No," I said. "The GPS says we're going the right way."

"This isn't the way I went."

"Sometimes in the modern age you can reach a destination using more than one route."

I did have to admit that I wished the GPS had an Avoid Scary Neighborhoods setting. The sun had set, and this was the kind of place where you really didn't want your car to break down after dark. I don't mean that in a cannibal-rednecks-with-chain-saws way, but muggers and drug dealers were worrisome enough. Most of the buildings seemed to be warehouses, and the ones that were actual businesses seemed to be closed. It was kind of strange and eerie.

"You don't have to be sarcastic," said Adam. "I'm making up for what I did."

"No, you're not. You're sitting in the back. You didn't even offer to pay for gas."

"I don't have any money."

"I know that. So how did you get the doll?"

Adam didn't reply.

"I'd really like to know how you got the doll," I said.

"What does it matter?"

"Oh, I don't know. I guess that if you robbed a convenience store to get the money to buy the doll, that's probably something I should know."

"It wasn't anything like that."

"Also, you never answered the essence question."

"Essence?" Kelley asked.

"He needed my essence to give the doll its power."

"Do you really want to know?" Adam asked.

"Yes."

"It's kind of gross."

"Tell me."

"Do you remember when you spent the night at my house a couple of weeks ago, and we decided to go swimming, and you asked if you could borrow some toenail clippers? Well, we'd never emptied the trash in that bathroom, and I was pretty sure that nobody else had clipped their toenails in there since then, so I dug out a few of them."

Kelley suddenly rolled down her window, as if she were going to be sick and didn't want to do it in my mom's car.

"Are you serious?" I asked.

I saw Adam nod in the rearview mirror.

"So you sat there, digging through the bathroom garbage in search of my toenails, and *still* thought this whole thing was a good idea?"

Adam shrugged.

"Our friendship is over."

"I figured."

Kelley still had her window down and was breathing in fresh (actually, not so fresh) air. This was really more of a windows-up kind of environment, but I didn't say anything.

Finally she rolled her window back up and turned around to look at Adam. "You," she said, "are vile."

"What is this? 'Pick on Adam' Day?"

"Yes. That's a great idea. Let's make a week out of it. You suck, Adam."

"Okay."

"You get negative points in every possible category of human existence."

"I'm not sure what that means, but okay."

"If you were lying in the desert miles from civilization and I had a bottle of water, I would—"

"Okay, okay," I said. "Everybody in this car understands that Adam sucks. We can let it go now."

We stopped at a red light. The street was empty except for a really skinny guy in baggy jeans and no shirt. He was on my side of the vehicle. His head was shaved, and his body was covered with approximately eighty billion tattoos. The centerpiece was Mickey Mouse doing something of which the Disney lawyers would almost certainly not approve.

He looked at us and smiled.

Not a "Hey, how ya doin', welcome to the neighborhood!" friendly smile. More of a sinister smile. I didn't like that smile at all.

He stepped off the sidewalk and approached the car.

"You should go," said Kelley.

"It's a red light."

"Just go."

"It's got a camera!" I'd been in favor of those controversial cameras when they were announced, because I had no plans to run red lights, but now I wished I was a registered voter with a say in the issue.

The man was right there. He tapped on my window. Not knowing what else to do, I rolled it halfway down.

"We don't want any marijuana," I told him, feeling like an absolute dork after I said it. I'm proud of the fact that I've never done drugs, but I could not possibly have said, "We don't want any marijuana," in a way that made me sound less cool.

He held out his palm. "Got a buck?"

"Oh yeah, sure." I started to reach for my wallet and then decided that this was not the best scenario in which to do such a thing. The guy didn't look homeless. He still looked pretty darn sinister.

I dug through the change next to the drink holder. "I've got, uh, twenty-five, fifty, sixty, sixty-five, seventy, seventy-one, seventy-two, seventy-three cents. Is that enough?"

"It'll do."

I tried to give him the change, but I was so nervous that I moved my hand too fast and I forgot that the window was halfway up and my hand smacked into the glass and coins flew everywhere.

Why was the light still red? This was the longest red light in the history of traffic.

"You gonna pick it up?" the guy asked.

The light turned green.

And then the gun came out.

I guess he had it in the back of his underwear, which is not where I would choose to keep a gun. Half of my brain shrieked, *Drive! Drive! Drive!* while the other half politely suggested that because the barrel of the gun was about twelve inches from my face, I should not make any sudden moves.

I froze.

Kelley froze.

I didn't dare take my eyes off the gun to peek in the rearview mirror, but I'm pretty sure that Adam froze too. Or fainted.

Time stood still, because time *loves* to make moments like this last as long as possible.

You're probably familiar with the concept of the unreliable narrator. When I read *Catcher in the Rye* in English class, we discussed how Holden Caulfield may not be telling us the truth about everything that happened. However, I can assure you that I am being one hundred percent accurate and honest when I tell you that the first thing I was able to say was, "Argh-ugh!"

I said, "Argh-ugh!" again to make sure my message was clear.

"Your phones," he said. "Drop your phones on the floor."

I quickly took my cell phone out of my pocket and tossed it on the floor. Fine. No problem. Happy to do it. If I wasn't willing to slam my foot on the accelerator, I certainly wasn't going to take the time to dial 911 with a gun in my face.

I heard the thumps as Kelley and Adam tossed their phones on the floor as well. (So if Adam had fainted, it was only briefly.)

"Now get out of the car," he said.

Aw, crap.

"*Get out!*" he repeated, kicking the door.

For a fraction of a second I thought the wisest thing to do would be to duck down, floor the accelerator, and hope for the best. But that essentially meant that I'd be ducking out of the way so that *Kelley* could get shot. I've admitted to a lot of dumb and/or selfish and/or cowardly things so far (see pretty much this entire book), but I wasn't going to let my girlfriend get shot.

Granted, if we both could have ducked at the same time, that would have been pretty awesome. Unfortunately, I couldn't think of any way to communicate to her that she should duck except for shouting, "Duck!" which probably would have given our plan away.

So I opened the door and got out of the car.

The carjacker kept the gun pointed at me. He was one twitchy guy. "Just stay calm," I told him, as if that piece of homespun advice might change his behavior.

"Both of you! Out!" he shouted, pointing the gun at Kelley and then at Adam. They both got out and put their hands in the air, even though the hands part hadn't been specifically requested.

Where were the other cars? Where were the helpful pedestrians? If I survived the night, I was definitely leaving a one-star review for that brand of GPS.

"Sir, I really need to get something out of the trunk," I said.

"No, you need to step out of the way before I put a bullet in your mouth."

"Please, it has no value. I just need—"

The guy pushed me out of the way. He got into the car, slammed the door shut, and sped off.

"Quick! Get the license plate!" Adam shouted.

"License plate? It's *my* car!"

This was beyond insane. My parents were going to absolutely freak. And the doll...what was going to happen to the doll? I didn't know much about the carjacking business, but I was pretty sure my mom's beloved automobile was headed for a chop shop. They could have a car taken apart in minutes.

Or what if he drove it into a lake? Would I drown?

What was I supposed to do? Find a pay phone, call the cops, and hope that nobody took an interest in the box with the weird symbols in the trunk?

And of course, I had oh-so-cleverly let the guy know that there was something important in there.

I had no choice. If I didn't want to, y'know, *die*, I had to get that doll back, no matter what.

"Come on!" I said as I began to chase after the car on foot.

CHAPTER 8

"What are you doing?" Kelley called after me.

"I have to catch him!"

"Are you crazy?"

I was probably at least a little. But I simply couldn't see a scenario in which the authorities handled this situation before somebody messed with the doll. I could just hear the carjacker: "My, what an interesting doll. Let me see if its legs can touch its head."

I guess there was also the possibility that he'd say, "Oh, look, a present for my darling daughter, who treats all of her possessions with the utmost of care," but I was leaning more toward the idea that really bad stuff would happen to the doll if I let it out of my sight.

The car turned the corner, leaving my sight.

I picked up my pace.

"Tyler!" Kelley shouted, running behind me. "For God's sake, stop it!"

"Don't come with me!" I shouted back. If the guy decided to point the gun out the window and start shooting, I didn't want either of them to get hit. (I was more concerned about Kelley's safety than Adam's.)

I was a good runner. I could catch it.

I could totally delude myself too.

No, no, just because he was a morally bankrupt carjacker didn't mean he wouldn't obey traffic laws. A really long red light, and I'd catch him.

I didn't have any specific plans for what I'd do if I actually caught up with him. Maybe he'd be so impressed with my dedication that he'd change his mind and give me the car back. "You're a feisty one! I like that. Here, have the keys. Sorry about the inconvenience."

At the end of the second block, I had a sudden moment of clarity, where the mysteries of the world were revealed to me, and my role in the universe was explained to me with six simple words: *You can't outrun a car, dumbass.*

I stopped.

I cursed. (S-word, f-word, s-word, d-word, s-word times three, f-word, and a z-word that I made up on the spot.)

I kicked a brick wall.

I said the z-word again in response to the pain that came from kicking a brick wall.

Kelley and Adam caught up to me. "What's the matter with you?" Kelley demanded. "Are you trying to get yourself killed?"

"I'm trying to make myself *not* get killed!"

"By chasing a man with a gun?"

"He's got the doll!"

"I know that! It doesn't mean you should go chasing after him like a lunatic!"

"What if they decide to torture the doll?"

"Why would they do that?"

"I don't know! He could give it to one of those rotten kids who wreck their dolls like in *Toy Story*! He could start burning off fingers!"

I was starting to hyperventilate, so I forced myself to take slow, deep breaths to calm down. I tried to think of happy images that did not involve each of my fingers blistering, blackening, and falling off.

"I'm going to die," I said.

"No, you're not."

"I am! There's no way they won't look in the trunk! There's a voodoo doll in there, and the lady who made it includes free pins, and they're probably going to poke it!"

"Why would they poke it? That's ridiculous."

"Because it's clearly a voodoo doll!"

"Nobody believes in voodoo!"

"If you found a voodoo doll, wouldn't you stick pins in it just for fun?"

"No."

"Adam?"

Adam nodded. "Yeah, I probably would."

"Nobody is going to stick pins in the doll," Kelley said.

"What if they just throw it away? What if it gets crushed in the back of a garbage truck? That's way worse than getting shot!"

"Depends where you got shot," said Adam. "If you got shot in the stomach, it would probably be better to just be crushed in a garbage truck."

"I don't want to die," I said, my voice cracking. "Not at all. I really don't want that."

"Well, we're not going to be able to catch him on foot, so we have to be reasonable about this," said Kelley. "We just have to find a phone and call the police."

Adam looked at her in horror. "I'm not going to jail!"

"I'm not reporting you! I'm reporting the stolen car! I know we're all freaked out about the voodoo doll, but do you really think we have a better way of getting it back?"

One block ahead, the just-stolen car came around the corner. We all stood there and stared as the carjacker drove up right next to us and stopped.

"Your mom called," said the guy, holding up my phone. "She sounded worried. I told her you were dead." He laughed and tossed the phone into the backseat. "Seeya!"

He sped off again.

I couldn't believe this. "He just—I can't—what the—how could—did you see—he just—"

Neither Kelley nor Adam had a response to this.

"I'm chasing him," I said, and I took off running again. Somebody who would cheerfully tell a teenager's mother that her child was dead would certainly poke a voodoo doll.

Much like your average dog, I still hadn't completely worked out what I was going to do if I succeeded in catching the car. But my adrenaline was pumping and my mind was racing and I felt like I could just yank his carjacking butt out of the vehicle, and toss him into a crosswalk signal. I knew that was unlikely to be the way this situation played itself out, but I simply wasn't willing to allow myself to become a pile of body parts.

Kelley shouted at me, but I kept going.

Nothing in the world was going to stop me from catching up with that car. *Nothing*.

Well, except for the microscopic patch of dirt that I tripped on, causing me to tumble forward and smash onto the ground. Though I was able to break my fall with my hands, saving myself from pulping my face against the cement, it still hurt.

Kelley and Adam ran up behind me and helped me to my feet. My palms were all scraped up, and my left knee stung.

"Please don't run anymore," Kelley requested.

She was right. Or maybe she wasn't right. One of those. Either way, it was clear that I was not going to suddenly become a superhuman crime fighter, which was very disappointing.

"It'll all be okay," said Kelley, giving me a hug. "I promise."

This weirded me out, because Kelley was not one to offer "things are gonna be just fine" sentiment in situations where things could be significantly less than fine. She pretty much called them as she saw them. I don't mean in a cruel "yes, the cancer *is* going to kill your grandmother" way, but if you said that you thought you weren't going to win at a swim meet, and she sized up the competition and agreed that you probably weren't going to win at the swim meet, she'd say that you probably weren't going to win at the swim meet, even though most other people would tell you that they thought you were going to win at the swim meet even if they didn't believe it.

For her to resort to "It'll all be okay, I promise," she had to be seriously stressed out.

Why did my elbow suddenly itch?

It was nothing. Phantom itch.

Another car turned onto the street, which was nice because it proved that we weren't in some sort of postapocalyptic wasteland.

A cab!

"Hey!" I shouted, waving my hands over my head. "Hey!"

As the cab approached us, Kelley and Adam joined in on the hand waving and hey shouting. The cab didn't seem to be slowing down, so I stepped out into the street in front of it. (It was half a block away, not inches. I wasn't going to go through all of this only to be hit by a taxi.)

The cab stopped, and the three of us rushed to the passenger-side door. I threw it open and leaned inside. The driver was a really muscular dude who looked about thirty, with long black hair that flowed over his shoulders. He could have passed for a romance novel cover model except that he was wearing a shirt.

"I'm not in service," he said.

"We really need your help," I insisted.

He shook his head. "I'm off duty! I'm gonna *party!*"

"Please! I'll double your fare!"

He looked at me suspiciously. "Where're you going?"

"We need you to try to follow a car."

"Car chase? Hell yeah! Get in!"

I hurriedly got in the front seat while Kelley and Adam got in the back. The cab shot forward before we'd even closed the doors.

"Which way did it go?"

I pointed ahead. "He turned right one block ahead."

The driver floored the gas pedal. I noticed a large number of aluminum cans on the floor.

"Fan of Red Bull?"

"Man, I chug that stuff like cold water in the desert! Woo! Woo!"

He spun around the corner so quickly that I was thrown against the door and Kelley was thrown against Adam, which I'm sure she didn't appreciate.

"What color car are we following? Blue? Red? Green? White? Taupe?"

"Silver."

"Silver! I love silver cars! Two door? Four door?"

"Four door."

"Hell yeah, four door! Oh, we'll find that silver four-door! We'll find it! Woo! Woo!"

I wished this cab came with a second seat belt. Or a shoulder bar like you'd get on a roller coaster.

"You look that way," said the driver, pointing out my window. "Girl in back, you look to the left. Guy in back, you look behind us. I'll just spin my head three-sixty and watch everywhere." He laughed way too loudly for the quality of the joke.

"Do you have a phone I could borrow?" I asked.

"Why?"

"I want to call the police."

"You wanna call the cops on me? Bite me."

"No, the guy who stole my car."

"You gonna let the cops ruin our fun? There's no party when the cops are around! Party! Woo! Woo! Woo!"

Getting in the cab, never the wisest course of action, was seeming like an even worse idea.

"It's really important that I get the car back," I said. "I just want a backup plan in case this car chase doesn't work."

"Oh, this is gonna work," said the driver. "When I've had this many Red Bulls, I get all extrasensory and stuff."

He sped through a red light. The camera flash went off.

"My bad," he said with a chuckle.

A couple of people were standing on the corner, looking like they might—I swear—be conducting some sort of illegal transaction involving ferrets. Maybe they were fake ferrets. I don't know. But a couple of ferrets were exchanged for an envelope. Then they watched us race by, looking at me as if there was something wrong with being in a speeding cab with a caffeine-overdosed driver.

"We're all going to die!" Adam predicted.

The cab ran over something small, but I am 97 percent sure it was not alive.

"Is that your car?" the cabbie asked, taking both hands off the wheel to point.

It was! My mom's car was about six blocks ahead, stopped at a red light.

"Yes! That's it! You're a genius!"

"Then hold on," he said. "I'm gonna run that thieving bastard right off the road!"

CHAPTER 9

There was a great deal of screaming after he said that.

Our driver clutched the steering wheel as if it were a struggling tiger, and though I can't prove it, I think he actually growled. I know for a fact that his eyes didn't really glow red, but if there were ever a time at which somebody's eyes would glow red, this was it.

Time once again seemed to move in slow motion. "IIIIIIII dooooooonnnnnn't thiiiiiiinnnnnk yooooooouuuuuu shouuuuuuuuld doooooooo thiiiiiiissssss!" I said.

The distance between the cab and my mom's car closed from six blocks to three blocks in about, oh, a quarter of a second.

"Nononononononononononono!" shouted Kelley and Adam at the same time, as if they'd rehearsed it.

Two blocks.

"Bad!" I screamed. "Badness!"

One block.

Then the cabbie slammed on the brakes. The tires screeched, and the cab spun into the opposite lane at a forty-five degree angle, and we all screamed some more.

"I decided I probably shouldn't do that," the driver explained.

"Thank you," I said.

"I'll just follow him at a reasonable pace."

He got back into the correct lane and proceeded to follow the car, which was going fast but not recklessly disregarding the law.

"Can I please borrow your phone?" I asked again. "I promise I won't call the police. My mom thinks I'm dead, and I need to tell her that I'm not."

"You're the third person today to say that."

"Seriously?"

"No. Gullible!" He punched me on the shoulder, then handed me his phone. "Here. Make it quick."

I stared at the phone for a moment.

"What's wrong?"

"I'm used to only picking her name from my contacts list. I'm trying to remember her actual number."

"Well, just scroll through recent calls. I've probably got your mom on there." He punched me in the arm again. "Kidding! Kidding! Gullible!"

My mom's car turned to the right and he followed, staying about a block behind.

The ten digits flashed into my mind. (I'm not going to share them here, because, no offense, you might be into prank calls.) I quickly dialed.

"Hello?" Mom answered, sounding frantic.

"Mom, it's me!"

"Tyler!"

"I've got to go, but everything's okay. I promise you I'm not dead." I hung up.

"Were you disappointed that I didn't ram him?" asked the driver.

"Not at all," I assured him.

"I can still make it happen."

"No, no. Just keep following him."

"He won't get away," said the driver. "Do you know what my vision is? Guess what my vision is."

"Twenty-twenty?"

"Not that good. I mean, I'm not a robot. But I can read pretty much any street sign. Go on, point to a street sign and see if I can read it."

"That's not necessary," I assured him. "Just follow the car."

"Are you being condescending?"

"No."

"Didn't think so. Just checking."

I didn't bother to look back at Kelley and Adam to gauge their expressions. I knew they were not smiling.

We continued the relatively low-speed chase for another couple of blocks, and then the carjacker stopped. A large metal sliding door opened to his right, he pulled into the garage, and the door closed behind him.

The cabbie drove up next to the door and stopped. I was surprised that he didn't ask if he should ram it.

I stared at the garage door, trying to figure out exactly what I should do.

"Did I ever tell you why I became a cabdriver?" asked the cabbie. "It's a long story but a fascinating one."

"I don't think we have time," I said.

"I'll tell you the short version. When I was three, my dad bought me a Matchbox car—"

"We really are kind of distracted right now."

"Doing what?"

"Figuring out how to get my car back."

"Oh, that car's not coming back. I'll tell you that right now. Anyway, it was a green Matchbox car, a Trans-Am, a kind of vehicle that you kids today don't really appreciate but that in my time was quite the—"

I tuned him out, which was not easy. What should I do? They were probably chop-shopping the car right now. At any moment the sadistic carjacker could find the box, and he *would* open it, and, okay, maybe he wouldn't start unraveling the doll right away. (I could imagine my skin unraveling, a long thin strip of flesh winding off of my arm until it was just veins and muscles.) But what if he tossed it in a garbage can? What if eighty tons of other garbage got poured on top of the doll at the dump?

I had to get the doll back. Now.

Or maybe I could send Adam to get it. Bribe him with a Snickers.

No, I had to do it.

I opened the door.

"What do you think you're doing?" Kelley asked.

"Saving my life." I got out of the cab.

"No!" Kelley opened the back door and got out as well. "He'll shoot you!"

"No, he won't."

"What are you going to do?"

"Knock."

"*Knock?*"

I nodded. "Knock."

"Uh, guys, don't leave me here," said Adam from the back-seat. "I don't have any money for the fare."

I gave Kelley a quick kiss on the lips. "I'll be fine," I assured her. "He has nothing to gain by shooting me. I can talk him out of it. Stay in the car. I'm going by myself."

"Don't do this. You don't have to."

I gave her another kiss. "Yes," I said, "I do." I have to admit that I said it in kind of a corny, melodramatic way, as if I were making some sort of noble sacrifice. Of course, I wasn't being a hero or anything—I was only trying not to have my fingers burned off one by one. Still, for that one moment, I felt as if Daniel-Day Lewis could play me in an Academy Award-winning motion picture.

"Get back in the cab," I told Kelley. "Nobody is going to shoot anybody, but if you do hear bullets, I won't be offended if you drive away."

Kelley let out an exasperated and heartsick sigh and then got back into the cab. She slammed the door shut. I suddenly decided that I could really use a hug before I went over to the garage door, but no…I'd wasted enough time already.

Then Adam got out of the car. "I'm coming with you," he said, his voice filled with bravery.

"No."

"I won't let you do this alone. Part of this is sort of my fault, and I'm going to stand by your side."

"Adam, my strategy involves talking. You're not good at it."

He looked hurt. "I can talk."

"Seriously, stay in the cab. I need you to protect Kelley."

Of course, Adam knew that I wouldn't put him in charge of protecting a bag of stale Cheetos, much less my girlfriend. He looked at the ground and shrugged. "All right. Shriek if you need me."

"I will. Get back in the car."

I walked over to the metal garage door. I was sick to my stomach, my head was pounding, at least eight different body parts were trembling, and I very much doubted that my bladder was going to operate at maximum efficiency. But what choice did I have?

I stood there for a few seconds, gathering my courage, and then I knocked.

This information comes from several different sources, mostly Wikipedia, which I know isn't completely reliable, but it's sure convenient.

Throughout his childhood, Gary Sheck's parents had said that one day he should open his own Italian restaurant. Nobody in the Sheck family was Italian, and in fact, the family had a long history of making fun of people with Italian accents, but nevertheless, that was the career path they encouraged. When he was sixteen, Gary took a job washing dishes at a local Italian restaurant, and that's when he discovered that being a professional dishwasher absolutely sucked.

Here's how it works: A customer complains to the server that the chicken on his fettuccine Alfredo is overcooked. The server says, "Oh goodness, I'm so sorry. I'll fix that right up, and it'll be no problem at all." The server goes back into the kitchen and informs the chef that the customer sent the chicken back because it was overcooked. Despite the server's assurance to the customer that it's no problem at all, it really *is* a problem, and the chef throws a minor temper tantrum. Of course, the chef can't come out into the dining area and punch the customer in the face or dump a bowl of spaghetti sauce on his head, so he yells at the server. The server can't yell at the chef or the customer, so to vent his or her frustration, the server yells at the dishwasher, who is entirely powerless and who had nothing to do with the overcooked chicken on the fettuccine Alfredo.

Gary quickly decided that he didn't like getting yelled at all day. *He* wanted to be the one yelling at people who weren't responsible for what they were getting yelled at for.

He vowed that he would work hard and rise through the ranks until he acquired the power he so desperately sought.

On his second day, when a server named Tom yelled at him because the customer complained about the insufficient intensity of tomato flavor in the lasagna, Gary hit Tom in the face with a large metal spoon and stormed out of the building, never to return to the restaurant business again.

Gary went to his parents and proposed the idea that instead of following the original plan of getting a job, he would pursue an alternate course of action where he did *not* get a job. Their counterproposal was a simple and straightforward scenario in which he *did* get a job immediately, perhaps something in retail.

Gary Sheck did not enjoy working retail.

On his second day, after an elderly woman waited until he'd completely rung up and bagged her purchases to reveal that she had a twenty-five-cents-off coupon, Gary raised his fist and was immediately fired. He walked home, unsure of whether he would have punched the old lady in the face or not.

The unanswered question really bothered him, so he walked around until he found another old lady, and then he punched her in the face.

That was infinitely more satisfying than owning an Italian restaurant.

After a few days of soul searching, Gary realized that his opportunities for hurting more people would be greatly increased if he focused on doing jobs that were illegal. He started with petty crimes—a mugging here, a grand theft auto there—and then, on his eighteenth birthday, as a present to himself, he shot a man.

It wasn't as much fun as he had thought it was going to be. The man died too quickly.

The next one took a lot longer. Gary was in a cheery mood for nearly three hours after that.

He joined a gang called Autopsy Report. By age twenty-five, he was their leader. He decided that Autopsy Report sounded more like the name of a band than a gang and changed it to the Maulers. He got reports that people were confusing it with "the Mallers" and assuming that their turf of terror was limited to shopping malls, so he changed it to the Red Shredders.

Gary knew that to instill fear in his enemies, he needed a trademark. So he became known for bashing his enemies to death with a brick. He was good at it.

By the time Gary was thirty, the Red Shredders had disbanded, but Gary and his five most loyal members stuck together and continued to commit crimes. Gary preferred crimes that were violent or at least destructive, but sometimes he settled for profitable, as with his lucrative auto-theft operation.

Gary was furious at the moment, because he'd told Scorp (the nickname for Scorpion, whose real name was Fred) not to bring in any more of these annoying, sensible, fuel-efficient cars. Scorp had apologized but didn't seem to really mean it, and he giggled when he told Gary how he'd stolen it from a teenage kid, and the kid's mom had called, and Scorp had told her the kid was dead.

Gary had to admit that that was pretty funny. Still, Scorp had disobeyed an order, so Gary threw him to the ground and kicked him in the side a few times.

Then they went to work dismantling the car.

"Hold up, hold up," said Gary, waving for everybody to be quiet. "Did you hear that?"

Shark (real name: Trevor), Blood Clot (Charles), Ribeye (also Charles) and Scorp all went silent.

"Somebody's knocking!"

Shark hurried over to the garage door and looked through the peephole. "Are you kidding me?"

"Is it the cops?" asked Blood Clot, who had never murdered a police officer but hoped to someday.

"Naw," said Shark. "It's a teenage kid."

"For real?" asked Scorp. "Blond hair?"

"Yeah."

Scorp let out a high-pitched laugh. "That's the kid I stole it from! Can you believe that?"

"You think that's funny?" asked Gary. "You lead him right back here to us, and you think it's something to laugh about? You gonna laugh in jail? Huh? You gonna have a nice big chuckle in jail?"

Scorp had received three separate black eyes (not that he had three eyes; his right eye had been blackened once and his left twice) and a cracked rib from answering Gary's rhetorical questions, so he said nothing.

Gary took out his gun. Ribeye and Blood Clot did the same.

"All right," said Gary. "Let him in."

I didn't know any of that when the garage door slid open. All I knew was that a big, frightening man grabbed me by the arm and pulled me inside, and then the garage door slammed shut, and then I had five guns pointed at me.

CHAPTER 10

Before this moment, the most guns I'd ever had pointed at me was one, and that was during the carjacking a few minutes ago. I wouldn't say that this was necessarily five times scarier, but it was at least three or four times scarier.

None of the criminals looked happy to see me.

I said the first thing that came to mind: "I'm not a cop!"

For a few seconds, they all just stared at me. Then Gary (who I did not yet know was Gary—I simply thought of him as muscular guy with goatee, black hair, and cruel eyes) chuckled. Scorp chuckled right after that, and they were quickly followed by Blood Clot, Shark, and Ribeye. Their chuckles never quite reached full-fledged laughter, nothing like what you'd see in a movie where the bad guys are all having a nice big guffaw, but they were all clearly amused by my comment.

"Not a cop, huh?" asked Gary. "They hiring a lot of terrified-looking teenage boys as cops these days?"

"I'm just saying…I'm not, y'know, wearing a wire or anything."

"Well, good." Gary patted me on the shoulder. "Good to

know. Because I've gotta say, when you came in here, I thought they'd sent in the marines."

The other guys chuckled some more.

I glanced over at my mom's car. The tires had already been removed, as had both doors. These guys were scumbag thieves, but I had to admire their efficiency. The trunk remained intact.

"What's your name?" Gary asked.

"Tyler."

"Tyler what?"

"Tyler Churchill."

"Well, Tyler Churchill, would you mind explaining to me exactly why the *hell* you knocked on our door?"

My mouth went completely dry, and it was difficult to speak. "You stole my mom's car."

"I stole nothing of the sort. I've been here all evening. Do you know what I do to people who falsely accuse me of wrongdoing?"

I shook my head.

He pressed the barrel of the gun against my forehead. "You can make an educated guess, right?"

I forced myself not to drop to my knees and start sobbing and begging for mercy. They hadn't opened fire on me with all five guns the second I stepped into their chop shop, so he had to be willing to discuss things.

I wondered if, possibly, this had been a bad idea.

"I didn't mean you," I said, my voice barely a whisper. I half-pointed to Scorp. "He took the car. It's…uh…right there."

"Oh, okay. You're saying that my *associate* stole your car. That's different. I agree with that. How old are you?"

"Sixteen."

"You packin'?"

"Heat?"

Gary looked at me as if glowing waves of stupidity were emanating from my forehead. "Yes, heat. Are you packing heat? Are you in possession of a firearm containing bullets with which you might try to shoot somebody?"

I vigorously shook my head.

"Ribeye, pat him down."

Ribeye set down his gun on the roof of the car and then gave me a not-very-gentle pat down that I thought might leave bruises. "Kid's clean," he announced. He walked back to retrieve his gun. I wished I'd stomped on his foot and then done a double backflip over to the car, where I could have grabbed his gun and shot all five of them before they had had a chance to react, but the window of opportunity was now closed.

"No gun, huh?" Gary asked me.

"No."

"Why would you show up without a gun? That sounds stupid to me. Very, very stupid. And I have a problem understanding acts of stupidity. Isn't that right, Blood Clot?"

"Yep," said Blood Clot. "You sure do."

"I'm always saying to myself, 'Why did that person do something so stupid?' And most of the time, I can't get a good answer. Which is why I'm so happy to have you here, right in the middle of one of the dumbest things I've ever seen somebody do. Explain it to me."

Now my mouth had gone so dry that I literally couldn't speak.

"Did you come in here thinking that my moral code would

not let me shoot a teenager? Is that it? I hope so, because I love irony." Gary grinned. "Don't I love irony, Blood Clot?"

"Oh yeah. You can't get enough of that ironic stuff."

Gary winked at me. And then his grin vanished, and his cruel eyes went dead serious. "It's extremely important that you don't think I won't kill you just because you're a kid. I'll kill a little girl and not lose a wink of sleep."

"I don't think you won't kill me," I said, finding my voice again. That didn't sound like what I'd actually wanted to say, but I wasn't completely sure what I *did* want to say and didn't correct myself.

"You call the cops?" Gary asked.

"No. He stole my phone."

"Your friends call the cops?"

"He stole their phones too."

Gary shrugged. "Makes sense. However, since it's no longer 1923, I'd guess that they wouldn't find it too difficult to get in touch with the authorities. Time's running out. Why are you here? Were you gonna steal your car back? It's gonna be hard to drive right now."

"I need something out of the trunk," I said.

"Seriously?"

"Yes."

"You're here because you forgot something in your *trunk*?"

"Yes, sir."

"Are you slow of mind?"

"I don't care what you do with the car. I mean, I do care— it's my mom's car, and she's going to go absolutely berserk—but I'm not going to try to stop you. Not that I could stop you, but I mean, you know what I mean."

"Could somebody please shoot him to stop the babbling?"

"No, no! All I'm saying is that if I could please have the box in the trunk, I'll get out of your hair and you can go back to what you were doing."

"Must be valuable," said Gary.

"Only sentimental value."

"Uh-huh. There's no sentimental value in the world worth getting shot over. Now you've gone and made me all curious. Scorp, open the trunk."

"We should clear out first," said Scorp.

"We'll clear out when *I* say it's time to clear out. That's what the secret passage is for. It'll be nice to get to use it again; it's been too long. Get that trunk open."

Scorp took out my set of keys and unlocked the trunk. He popped the lid, revealing the small wooden box.

"Nice box," said Gary. "I like the symbols. Good tattoo ideas."

I wasn't sure whether to thank him for the compliment or not. I decided on not.

As Scorp took the box out of the trunk, it occurred to me that a much better plan would have involved Kelley and Adam setting up some sort of distraction at a designated time. So Scorp would pick up the box, and he'd be *juuuuust* about to open it when a huge explosion knocked all five thugs off their feet. From there, it would be the aforementioned matter of acquiring one of the guns and shooting it five times. Then the taxi would plow right through the garage door. No problem.

Gary picked up the box. "Pretty light for something full of cash."

"It's not cash. It's a doll."

"A doll?" Gary rattled the box.

I gasped and literally clutched at my heart, which felt like it skipped a beat and then did six hundred beats in a half-second to compensate.

"Whoa, whoa, what's your problem?" Gary asked.

"It's fragile!"

Gary set the box on the cement floor and then lifted the lid. "It *is* a doll."

"Right. Just a doll. My grandmother made it. On her deathbed."

"She made you a doll on her deathbed?"

"Yes," I said. "That's why it's not a very well-made doll. It's doesn't have any actual value, not even on *Antiques Roadshow*, but my mom will be heartbroken if something happens to it."

"And you think I look like the kind of person who cares if your mother is heartbroken?"

"There's no reason not to give it back to me," I said.

Gary lifted the doll out of the box by its arm. "What's inside it?"

"Nothing."

"There's something inside. I don't care if your grandmother was the homemade meatloaf queen of the United States, you wouldn't be doing this for a doll. Ribeye, get me a knife."

"Please!" I said. "Don't cut it open."

"I ain't got a knife," said Ribeye.

"Blood Clot, get me a knife."

"I don't have one either," Blood Clot admitted. "I've got a screwdriver."

"Screwdriver's fine," said Gary.

Blood Clot tossed him a screwdriver. Gary moved his hand out of the way, and the tool clattered onto the floor.

"Don't *throw* it at me! *Hand* it to me! Do you want that thing to go right through my palm? What's the matter with you?"

"I thought you'd catch it."

"That's how people get hurt, moron. Now pick it up."

Blood Clot sheepishly walked over to where the screwdriver had fallen. He picked it up, handed it to Gary, then walked back to where he'd been standing.

"I swear to you there's nothing inside the doll," I said. "It's really important that you not cut it open."

"Why?"

"It just is."

"I don't know why you're getting so bent out of shape over this doll. You realize that I'm going to kill you, right? You've captured my interest and all that, but this is gonna end with you getting a bullet in the head. Bloody corpses don't care much about dolls."

"Please, I'll do anything," I said. "I'll steal cars for you. I'll mop the floors." Yeah, I was no James Bond in the face of danger, but considering the circumstances, I think I could've been handling myself much worse.

"That's a very tempting offer, but I think ol' Ribeye would be disappointed if I let somebody else mop up the gore." He picked up the doll and placed the tip of the screwdriver against its chest.

"*Voodoo doll! Voodoo doll!*" I shouted. I'd meant to be more articulate than that, but I hoped that got the point across.

"Say what?"

"It's a voodoo doll," I said, more calmly.

"It does look like a voodoo doll," said Gary. "How about that?"

"So you can understand why I don't want you to rip it open with a screwdriver."

Gary let out a high-pitched laugh. "This is a voodoo doll of *you*? Aw, man, that's some bad luck, huh? Hey, Blood Clot, didn't you try to make a voodoo doll of your ex-wife that one time?"

"Naw, man."

"Yeah, yeah, you did. You were all like 'I'll teach her to come home from work early and catch me with that tramp,' and you were jabbing pins into a SpongeBob SquarePants doll."

"Wasn't me."

"Yeah, it was. No, wait, it was Ribeye. Hey, Ribeye, didn't you try to make a voodoo doll of your ex-wife that one time?"

"Ex-girlfriend."

"Right, right. How did that work out for you?"

Ribeye shrugged. "I don't know. As far as I know, she didn't complain about any pain, but we weren't living together anymore, so I wasn't around to say for sure. Made me feel better, though."

Gary slowly slid the tip of the screwdriver across the chest of the doll. "You're sweating a bit there, buddy," he said to me. "You really believe in this thing, don't you?"

"Yes," I said.

"You're serious. You're *deranged* but serious. What do you think is gonna happen when I jab this screwdriver in here?"

"Hopefully nothing."

"Oh, hey, there are a few pins in the box. How convenient." He tossed the screwdriver back at Blood Clot. "No sense wasting all of the fun on gouging your chest out right away, huh?"

Blood Clot picked up the screwdriver and glared at him.

I was in a state of absolute panic, but what could I do? Should I attack him? That seemed risky. Should I wait around and hope that he was only kidding? Though I hated to not be proactive, there were still multiple guns pointed at me.

Gary selected a nice long pin with a light blue head. "This one is perfect, don't you think? I've always liked the color blue. Especially this particular shade. Now where should I poke it? Hmmm. Decisions, decisions…"

"Black magic is not something you should take lightly," said Ribeye. "There are forces in this universe more powerful than anything you can imagine, things we cannot see with our regular five senses, and you shouldn't be taunting them."

"Shaddup."

"I agree with Ribeye," said Scorp. "That voodoo stuff, it can be nasty. What if all of this playing around gets you a voodoo priestess coming after you? That what you want?"

"Get lives, all of you," said Gary. "I'm just having some fun with Paranoid Boy here. Now where, where, oh where should I stick this pin?"

What would you do in this situation? I'm not actually soliciting advice—it's too late for that—but I'm curious. The most common answer is probably "I would never have gotten into this jam in the first place, because I wouldn't have messed with the voodoo doll, even under peer pressure," and the second most common is probably "Well, I at least wouldn't have knocked on the damn garage door!"

But let's pretend you did do all that. What would you do now?

The way I looked at it, here were my options:

1. Faint. *Advantages:* Easy to do. Everything is less scary when you're unconscious. *Disadvantages:* Could hit head on floor. Would probably be dead before I woke up.

2. Scream for help. *Advantages:* Easy to do. A kindly individual might hear and help. *Disadvantages:* 99.9997 percent chance that Gary & Co. would shoot me before I finished the first scream.

3. Acquire invulnerability. *Advantages:* Bullets would bounce off of me, and the voodoo doll would be powerless against me. *Disadvantages:* Unlikely to happen in the next few seconds.

4. Try to fake him out. *Advantages:* If it worked, I might not die. *Disadvantages:* I was not immediately sure how to go about such a thing.

All of my options pretty much sucked raw eggs through a straw, so I went with the fourth one. "What makes you so sure that doll isn't of *you?*" I asked.

Gary raised an eyebrow. "Are you trying to fake me out?"

"That doll needs somebody's essence to work. By touching it, you've transferred your essence into it. You jab a pin in there, you might as well be jabbing a pin right into your own brain."

"That's not how voodoo dolls work."

"Are you *sure?*"

"I'm comfortable with my decision," he said, jabbing the pin into the corner of the doll's foot.

CHAPTER 11

Oh yeah, I screamed.

Here's what it felt like: Imagine that somebody (probably not a close friend) took a small pair of garden shears, opened the blades, pressed them against the little toe on your left foot, and then closed the shears with a *crunch*. The corner of my white shoe instantly turned red, and it felt all squishy inside, and the pain was beyond belief.

All of the thugs looked completely shocked.

"Look at his foot!" shouted Blood Clot, pointing as I fell to my knees. "That ain't natural!"

"Ow!" I screamed. "Ow! Ow! Ow!"

I couldn't be completely sure, but it really felt like I was missing a toe. A toe! I'd lost a toe! I only had nine toes! Okay, yeah, this wasn't anywhere near as bad as losing an entire leg…but I'd lost a freaking toe!

"Shoot him in case he's a witch!" Blood Clot shouted, his voice filled with panic.

"Nobody shoots anybody until I say so!" Gary pointed the doll at me as if it were a gun. "Get that shoe off."

I'd mastered the art of tying and untying my shoes over a decade ago, but now I was having serious difficulty with the whole bunny-going-through-the-hole thing. I finally managed to get the shoe off and tossed it aside, revealing a red, drenched sock. I still wasn't entirely sure that my toe was completely off, although if it wasn't, there was a small rock in my sock.

"Ditch the sock!" said Gary.

I yanked off the sock. Four of my toes were perfectly fine, but the fifth one was just sort of…well, not there anymore, except for a tiny piece of bone.

"That is messed up," said Blood Clot.

"Let me see the toe," said Gary.

"You think I'm *faking* this?" I wailed.

"I said let me see it!"

I picked up the sock and shook it a few times until my toe dropped out. I whimpered. I sniffled. I did not, however, hug it to my chest and sob, so that's a point in my favor.

"Hol…lee…crap," said Gary. "It worked. It actually worked."

"Are voodoo dolls supposed to do that?" asked Ribeye. "I thought it was just supposed to make his foot, like, hurt or something."

"Where'd you get this?" asked Gary, waving the doll at me.

"It was a gift." I really wished that blood would stop coming out of the place where my toe had once been.

"Where'd they get it?"

"None of your business!" I'm no martyr, but I sure wasn't going to tell this guy where Adam had gotten the doll. If Gary used a vast collection of dolls to assassinate national leaders so that he could rule the world, it wasn't going to be because of any address *I* gave him.

"I wonder how much of a waterfall I can get if I stick this in your neck?" asked Gary.

So this was what it felt like to be moments away from death. It sucked about as much as I'd expected.

As Gary touched the pin to the doll's neck, I retreated into a glorious, wonderful fantasy world.

"Hey, Adam," I say, narrating in present tense for no particular reason, "did you throw away that voodoo doll like I asked?"

"I couldn't," he says. "We live in a world where voodoo dolls don't exist. Nobody has ever heard of them. They cause no trouble for anybody."

"What a fantastic universe!" I say, dancing around as sparkly colored lights follow me and upbeat music plays. "I want to live here forever!"

"And you can!" says Kelley with a merry laugh. "Forever and ever and ever and ever!"

"Changed my mind," said Gary, moving the pin away from the doll's neck. "Why end the fun so soon?"

He jabbed it into the doll's foot again.

The fourth toe on my left foot shot off like a bottle rocket, leaving a trail of red mist instead of smoke.

It struck Blood Clot right in the face.

"Aw, *bleagh!*" Though it hit him in the cheek and not the mouth, he spat a couple of times and wiped his mouth off on his sleeve. "What the hell, dude?"

I screamed some more.

"That was awesome!" Gary shouted. "Let's try that again! Open wide!" (I couldn't hear exactly what he was saying with all of the screaming I was doing, but I think that's a pretty accurate guess.)

Eight toes. I only had eight toes. Did this mean I'd have to start wearing narrower socks?

Suddenly, the garage door did not burst open and no reinforcements arrived to save me.

I clutched at my leaking foot and howled like one of those howler monkeys in South America.

"Stop doing that," said Blood Clot.

"I just lost two toes!" I shouted. "What else do you want me to do?"

"Not you! The screaming's okay." Blood Clot pointed his gun at Gary. "Knock it off."

"I'm *sure* you don't have a gun pointed at me," Gary said, his voice filled with rage.

"This is one of the most amazing discoveries of the twenty-first century, and you're using it to play around and blow off toes. I can't stand here and let that happen."

"Ribeye, kill that traitor."

Ribeye hesitated for a moment and then pointed his gun at Gary as well. "Sorry, dude. We really should be using this for something more ambitious."

Scorp pointed his gun at Blood Clot. "Who do you think

you are? You throw down that gun, or I will drop you where you stand!"

Shark pointed his gun at Gary. "Screw all of you guys!" he said. "None of you ever acknowledge me! You probably forget that I'm even here, and I'm tired of it! I'm just as important a part of this gang as anyone, and all I want is a little respect, okay? Is that so much to ask?"

Gary dropped the voodoo doll. None of my bones broke when it hit the floor, which was nice. "Listen to me, Blood Clot," he said. "You have exactly five seconds to lower your gun, or I'm going to kill you with my bare—"

Blood Clot shot Gary in the chest.

Scorp fired, missing Blood Clot.

Ribeye turned his gun on Scorp.

Shark fired, hitting Gary in the chest a second time.

Blood Clot turned his gun on Scorp.

Ribeye fired, missing Scorp.

Scorp fired, grazing Blood Clot's ear.

Blood Clot fired, grazing Scorp's ear in almost the exact same place his own ear had been grazed. Honestly, you'd think they'd planned it out.

A few more bullets were fired with nobody getting hit.

Gary dropped to the floor.

Ribeye shot Scorp right in the freaking *eyeball*, which made my wallowing about my two missing toes seem kind of petty.

Scorp dropped to the floor.

Ribeye shot Blood Clot in the chest. His motive was not entirely clear to me, but I'm sure he had a good reason.

Blood Clot pulled his trigger a couple of times as he fell, but he was out of bullets.

Shark fired a bullet that I assume had to have been meant for Ribeye, because he was the only one left, but it was so far off the mark that I was a little embarrassed for him.

Ribeye fired at Shark, missing.

Shark fired at Ribeye, also missing.

They fired simultaneously, and I swear I'm telling the truth when I say that their bullets struck each other in midair and…Okay, no, that didn't happen. They just missed each other again.

Ribeye shot Shark in the foot, and he went down screaming.

Shark blew a couple of holes in the ceiling, apparently just to prove that he could hit *something*.

Ribeye shot Shark in one of the three places that I would least want to get shot.

And then Ribeye fired a bullet that definitely, positively, inarguably, with 100 percent certainty killed Shark. It was pretty disgusting.

Until today, I had never seen a dead body, and now I was in a garage with four freshly murdered ones. I knew that if I were to ever write about this experience, I'd have to do so with an inappropriately lighthearted tone to help me cope with the horrors I'd witnessed.

Ribeye pointed his gun at me.

"Aw, c'mon, seriously?" I asked.

"Seriously."

"Why would you need to shoot me?"

"Because there are four corpses in this room and you know

who made them. One corpse, not such a big deal, but I can't have you squealing about four of 'em."

I tried to scoot away from him, even though I knew it wasn't going to be very helpful. "I won't say a word," I promised. "I'll say I shot off my own toes! I'll tell everybody you were a hero, but I'll say you were a mystery man whose face I never got to see, that you were always in shadow!"

"Stop talking," Ribeye said, and then he pulled the trigger.

I was going to put a chapter break here, so that you might think I died and that the book was going to suddenly switch to Kelley's point of view as she set off on her quest to avenge my murder, but I figure a couple of hours after this is published, the Internet is going to be filled with spoilers saying that I don't die at the end of Chapter 11, so why bother?

What really happened is that he pulled the trigger and the gun didn't shoot anything, because it was out of bullets. Kind of a cop-out, I know, but sometimes real life doesn't follow the rules of good storytelling.

My foot was bleeding a little less than it had been immediately after my toes had come off, though this fact wasn't all that reassuring. Also, I'd been in here for quite a while, so what exactly were Adam and Kelley doing? Shouldn't somebody have stopped by to at least check on me?

"Please," I said. "Don't kill me. You could be rich."

"How?"

"The doll has more power. A lot more."

Ribeye raised an eyebrow. "Like what?"

"It can grant wishes."

On a scale of one to ten of "Awesome Ways to Convince a Thug That He Shouldn't Kill You Because a Voodoo Doll Has More Power Than What He's Already Seen," that ranked about a two. It was better than shoving a finger up my nose and saying "Durrrr…I dunno!" but not by much.

There was a knock on the garage door.

It was sort of a timid knock. Probably not the police with a battering ram.

"You've lucked out," said Ribeye. "If you can get a sock tied around that foot in the next few seconds, you can come with me."

I grabbed my bloody sock and tied it around my foot, pulling it as tight as I could. Ribeye picked up the doll and spat on Gary's dead body.

"Think you can walk?" he asked.

I nodded. As bad as my left foot hurt, at least I still had 60 percent of my toes left, and the ones remaining were the three biggest.

"Then let's go to the secret passage."

CHAPTER 12

Because Ribeye was the only one left, I guess I should probably give you a physical description. He was not a handsome gentleman. It wasn't the scars—those were actually kind of cool—or even his basic facial structure that made him so unattractive. A lot of it was his hair, which looked like it hadn't been washed for the past six to eight weeks, unless he'd recently dunked it in a barrel of bacon grease.

His eyes, nose, and mouth were where they were supposed to be and perfectly fine in size and shape. His facial hair was…uh, *sporadic*. Look, I'm not saying that I'm a beard-growing superstar. I was rocking the whole "peach fuzz on the upper lip" style for a while. But when you grow out of your teenage years, if your facial hair grows in weird, random clumps around your face, it's time to consider that perhaps the clean-shaven look is best for you.

Also, he constantly had his face all scrunched up in a grimace, which didn't do much for him.

He was about six-one, six-two. Maybe 180, 190. Eyes that were a light shade of hazel. Teeth that were also a light shade of hazel. His neck was muscular but not so muscular that you'd see him and say, "Whoa! Look at that guy's neck!" His feet were size eleven-and-a-half, I'd estimate, and I don't know how ring sizes work, but I'd guess that he was about a large. He wore work boots, faded blue jeans, red boxer shorts that protruded from the top of his jeans—not in that style where people walk around with half of their underwear visible, just enough where you could tell it was less a fashion choice than him simply needing a belt—and a red T-shirt with a picture of somebody who was either a music star or a world leader. (I didn't recognize him.)

When Ribeye smiled, he got a little crinkle over his left eye. It wasn't adorable or anything, although I guess one of his close relatives might have thought it was kind of cute. His left ear was pierced, and he wore a simple silver star, which surprised me because I would have expected him to be more of a "skull earring" kind of guy or maybe a gun or a dollar sign, something more closely associated with a life of crime. The star earring must have been a gift, perhaps from his grandmother or a favorite aunt, and though it didn't reflect his true personality, he still wore it to express his love, because even somebody like Ribeye has those he loves and who love him in return.

Finally, his chin was kind of pointy. But not too pointy.

"Stand up," said Ribeye.

I got to my feet, which didn't hurt as badly as I expected. I mean, it sure didn't feel like I was walking on a fluffy cloud, but the pain wasn't as intense as it could've been. I guess you don't need your toes as much as you'd think.

Then I stumbled and fell. The pain was a little more intense now.

"I said stand up," said Ribeye, pointing his gun at me.

Yeah, yeah, we both knew the gun was empty. It's still scary to have a gun pointed at you. I got back up.

There was another timid knock at the garage door.

"Let's go," said Ribeye, shoving me forward. We hurried to the back of the garage. In the rear corner, he bent down and pulled aside a small rug, exposing a wooden trapdoor. He lifted the door, revealing a metal ladder that led down into complete darkness. Without waiting for Ribeye to say something threatening (for example, "Climb down there before I harm you!") I began to climb down the ladder.

This didn't seem to be a particularly foolproof escape plan, because I'd left a trail of bloody footprints and I didn't see a way to get the rug back over the door after we closed it, not to mention that modern police officers tend not to be flummoxed by the rug-over-the-trapdoor trick. But hey, if Ribeye wasn't concerned, I wasn't going to be. It didn't take long to get to the bottom of the ladder, and then we were cast into complete darkness as Ribeye shut the door above us. There was a loud beep that sounded like an alarm system being activated.

He climbed down and then poked me in the back. "Walk."

I walked. The floor was still cement, but it was quite a bit wetter and slimier than the cement floor of the garage, and the aroma suggested that we weren't as far from the sewer as one might hope. This couldn't be very sanitary for my foot.

Though I'd just decided not to be concerned about the foolproof nature of Ribeye's escape plan, my curiosity quickly became too much to bear. "Won't they know where we went?" I asked.

"Don't talk," he said.

I didn't talk for a few seconds. But I really wanted to know, and quite honestly, if Ribeye hadn't killed me yet, was asking a simple question going to be the act that pushed him over the edge?

"They'll know where we went," I said.

"I've got it covered," Ribeye assured me.

"How?"

"Good old-fashioned booby trap. Anybody lifts the door to come down after us, *kaboom*. Their upper lip and lower lip won't be part of the same mouth anymore."

I stopped walking for a moment until Ribeye smacked me on the shoulder to get me moving again. Were Kelley and Adam really headed into a trap? Should I shout out a warning?

"Kelley!" I shouted. "Don't—"

The punch to the back of the head shut me up. I fell to the ground, my face landing in a very shallow but bacteria-rich pool of what may have once been water.

"Try that again, and I'll rip the doll's head off," Ribeye said.

I had no reason to believe he was lying. I got back up, coughed a few times, and then resumed walking.

Something scampered over my foot.

Something else followed it.

"You…you may have a rat problem down here," I said.

I hadn't spent much time in the company of rats, so I didn't realize until that very moment that they scared the hell out of me, at least when I was walking in a pitch-black sewer tunnel.

I forced myself to keep walking so that Ribeye wouldn't hit me again.

Surely, these weren't filthy, disease-carrying rats. They were cute rats, the kind you'd find in a pet store. They probably had pink bows around their necks. Nothing to worry about. Nothing at all.

I smacked into a wall.

"Turn right," said Ribeye.

My nose hurt but didn't seem to be bleeding. I turned right and continued to walk, holding my arms out in front of me. My good foot slipped in some slime, and I lost my balance for a split second, but I saved myself from taking a comical spill.

I hadn't heard any explosions or screaming. Hopefully, if Kelley and/or Adam did come into the garage, they realized that when you see bloody footprints leading into a dark pit, it's best to go in the opposite direction.

More scurrying next to my feet.

Think of other things, I told myself. Bunnies. Goldfish. Pugs. Flowers. Amusing monkeys. Snoopy.

There had to be thousands of rats down here. Or maybe just the three. Somewhere between three and thousands. It didn't matter. Even one rat—even *half* a rat—was too many.

What diseases did rats carry? Rabies? The Black Death?

No, no, no, I had to think positive. These were charming rats, like Remy the Rat, who wanted nothing more than to become a master chef in a five-star restaurant.

On today's fine dining menu, teenager flesh! Nom nom nom!

I kept walking.

I didn't feel it with my hands, but my face went right through a great big spider web. I frantically wiped it off of my cheeks and out of my hair. Don't you hate walking through spider webs?

Don't you hate how your neighbors see you and it looks like you've just suddenly decided to start clawing at your face for no reason? And you feel like you should go over and explain that no, you didn't have a fit of insanity, you just walked through a web, but instead you keep walking and hope that they didn't notice? I hate that.

There was something crawling on the back of my neck.

I yelped and slapped at it.

"What's the matter with you?" asked Ribeye.

"There's a tarantula on me!"

Okay, it couldn't really be a tarantula, but it was a huge spider, and I had to get it off me before it laid eggs in my hair, which would immediately hatch into millions of other spiders. I smacked all over the back of my head until the spider scurried onto my fingers, at which point I yipped like a poodle and shook my hands as rapidly as I could.

Nothing seemed to be crawling on me anymore.

Was that a hissing sound?

I was definitely imagining things. There were no snakes down here.

"Are there snakes down here?" I asked.

"Are you an idiot? Keep walking."

I bet there *were* snakes down here. Snakes and spiders and rats and alligators. It wouldn't surprise me if there was a much deeper puddle ahead with a great white shark. Oh, this sewer sucked.

I was so distracted by the deadly wildlife that I'd forgotten to keep my arms extended, so I smacked into another wall. My nose still wasn't bleeding. I have a resilient nose.

"Out of the way," said Ribeye, shoving me aside. I heard some metal rattling and then some cursing and then some more metal rattling and then a curse word that even people who curse a lot don't usually say.

"What's wrong?" I asked.

"I think Gary locked the door."

"Is that bad?"

"What do you think?"

Because there were snakes, spiders, rats, alligators, sharks, and probably a mountain lion down here, I guessed that it was probably pretty bad.

More rattling, more cursing, and then a few loud kicks.

"Can I help?" I asked. I wasn't volunteering to kick (remember, toe issue), but I certainly didn't want to be trapped down here.

"You can help by shutting up," said Ribeye, kicking the door a few more times. He sounded like my mom when he said that, but I didn't share this with him.

With the next kick, something definitely gave.

And then a little voice in my head said, *Gosh, Tyler, I hate to bother you, but by any chance did you notice that the homicidal thug who kidnapped you is sort of distracted at the moment? I don't want to be pushy or anything; I just thought it was kind of interesting that if you were inclined to make a move that would save your life, right now might be a pretty good time to consider it. Again, not trying to tell you what to do; only making an observation. Thanks!*

The nonexistent voice in my head was right. Unless my plan to escape was to wait for a magic fairy to make everything all right, I needed to act, and now was the time. Though I had no weapons, it's not like I was some scrawny weakling. I could hit hard.

I balled my hands together into a mighty double fist and then bashed him on the back of the head.

He fell.

Then he got right back up, grabbed me by the throat, and squeezed.

I kneed him in the hip, which was not where I was aiming.

He let go of my throat.

I tried to bite him but didn't come anywhere close.

He dropped something in the dark. It didn't clatter, so I was pretty sure it was the doll and not the gun. I hoped neither of us would step on it.

Ribeye did something else in the dark that sounded very much like he was taking a switchblade knife out of his pocket and snapping open the blade. You can guess how happy that sound made me.

He took a swing at me. I dodged backward, slipped on something slimy with my bad foot, and fell on my butt.

My hand came down on a rat, which let out a horrifying squeak as something inside of it snapped. I pulled my hand away from it in revulsion. The creature, twitching and rolling, bumped into my leg.

"I'm gonna cut you up," said Ribeye.

It was true. I was going to be sliced and diced, and there was nothing I could do about it...

...well, except throw the rat.

I grabbed the squirming, squealing rodent by the tail and flung it at Ribeye. From his startled reaction, I'm pretty sure it hit him in the face. He responded with much more panic than I'd shown when I walked through the spider web.

I'd only expected a second or two of distraction, but Ribeye continued to flail around and bat at himself, leading me to believe that the half-crushed rat had gone down the front of his shirt.

I like to think that it bit him over and over as it slid down his chest. He sure acted like it did. Heh heh.

So far in this book, I've shared a bunch of things I've done that weren't very smart, and I'll share a few more before it's over. However, I'm pleased to say that I did not waste the rat-down-the-shirt opportunity. I advocate peaceful solutions to conflict whenever possible, and there are very few circumstances under which it's okay to bash somebody's head against the wall. I feel that this was one of them. I'm not saying that you should expose somebody's brain or anything like that, but if you're following the Moral Code of Tyler Churchill, a few slams to help ease them into dreamland is acceptable.

I still couldn't see anything, but the sound effects were *Wham! Wham!* "Aaah!" *Wham! Squeak. Thud.*

Ribeye and the rat went silent.

I quickly picked up the voodoo doll. I had never been happier to pick up a sewage-tainted doll in my entire life. I sighed with relief. All of my problems were solved, except for the one about my girlfriend and (former) best friend possibly walking into a deadly booby trap.

I ran back through the tunnel the way I had come. It hurt.

I reached the ladder without slipping on slime or being attacked by an alligator. "Is anybody up there?" I shouted.

"Tyler?" It was Adam.

Wow. He'd actually come to save me. I couldn't believe it.

"Adam! Don't come down here! Don't touch the trapdoor!"

"Did you know that there are dead bodies all over the place?" He sounded more than a little distressed by this observation.

"Yes, I did! Just go back outside and wait for me. I know another way out."

"Is any of this blood yours?"

"Yeah, but it's okay. I got the doll."

"I think I'm going to pass out."

"You'll be fine."

"I'm really not feeling good, Tyler. I think I need to lie down."

"Fine. Do what you need to do. Just don't come down here."

I turned and ran back through the tunnel. It hurt again.

Ribeye had not regained consciousness. I listened for a moment to confirm that he was breathing and then bashed the door with my shoulder. Three hits, and it flew open. A small light bulb hung from the ceiling, revealing a ladder leading up.

I quickly climbed it, pushed open another trapdoor, and emerged next to a huge pile of metal scrap. I was in a small junk-yard. I shut the trapdoor and looked around. There were rusty automobiles and random piles of unidentifiable metal every-where, along with a small wooden building that I assumed was where they rang up your purchases.

The trapdoor was camouflaged on top with a layer of fake dirt that perfectly blended with the real dirt. When I closed the lid, you couldn't tell anything was there.

The whole junkyard was surrounded by a tall wire fence, but

it didn't seem to be electrified, so that wouldn't pose too much of a problem.

The Rottweiler, on the other hand...

CHAPTER 13

It came running around the largest scrap heap, furiously barking. There was no way I could get the trapdoor back open in time, so I considered my options.

Option One: Try to—

Before I could finish considering my first option, the Rottweiler knocked me to the ground and pulled the doll out of my hand.

I expected all of my toes, fingers, and assorted facial features to jettison from my body at once. Fortunately, I didn't feel an urge to shriek in unbearable agony, so apparently the dog's teeth hadn't punctured the doll yet. The dog ran off about twenty feet, then turned around, as if daring me to fight it for the prize.

"Good doggie," I said. "Please don't bite down."

The Rottweiler shook its head back and forth like it was drying itself after an unwanted bath.

I immediately felt a wave of dizziness beyond anything I'd experienced in my life. My vision went completely blurry. My legs lost their ability to hold up the top half of my body, and I collapsed to the ground. The entire world was spinning, spinning, spinning.

I knew that I needed to fight through this, but the best I could do was dig my fingers into the ground and hope it was enough to keep the earth from flinging me off its surface deep into outer space, where I'd smack into Jupiter.

I threw up. More than once.

I was so dizzy that I didn't really even care what the dog was doing. It was like the time when I was a kid, when I got on the chair in my dad's office and just spun and spun and spun and spun until I fell off onto the floor and hit my head and had to go to the hospital, except a million times worse. I didn't believe in interdimensional hyperspace vortex portals, but if I did, this felt like the way to open one.

I tried to push myself up, but my body said, "Nah, I don't think so," and kept me down.

When was this going to stop?

Maybe it was never going to stop. Maybe I was going to spend the rest of my life in this dizzy, spinny, pukey state.

The dog hadn't yet ripped out my throat or apparently the throat of the doll. My initial thought was that he wasn't a very good guard dog if those throats remained intact, but at the same time, I certainly wouldn't be stealing anything from the junkyard on my way out, so maybe he was perfectly fine. I'd figure it out later when the Tilt-A-Whirl in my brain stopped.

The world was spinning a little less quickly. Or else I was just holding on to the earth better.

I thought I heard somebody calling my name, although they may have also been calling for Orville Redenbacher.

Okay, the planet was definitely slowing down. I could make

out some shapes. I couldn't identify these shapes, but at least now I knew there were shapes in my general vicinity.

"Tyler?"

Who was that? A leprechaun?

"Tyler!"

It sounded like a girl. I hoped it was a hot leprechaun.

Now there was an annoying clanging sound, as if somebody were rattling a chain-link fence. I tried to remember if I'd seen a chain-link fence recently. There was that one around the junkyard where that dog had stolen my voodoo doll, but that was years ago, wasn't it?

I could see that there were colors attached to these shapes. One of the shapes was a black panting one that kind of looked like a mean dog. The other looked like a pile of scrap metal.

Junkyard. I was lying in the junkyard.

"Tyler!"

Yep, it was a girl. Adam? No, wait, Adam wasn't a girl. I knew that voice. Kelley.

I looked over. Kelley was standing outside of the fence, maybe ten feet away. Or two hundred feet away. It was still hard to calculate distance.

"Are you okay?" Kelley asked.

"Not great."

"Can you get up?"

With some effort, I got myself into a sitting position. My head felt like it weighed about forty pounds, but I was finally able to hold it upright.

"Do you think you can climb the fence?" Kelley asked.

I studied the fence. Maybe with an escalator I could.

"Do I have to do it now?" I asked. It sounded like somebody else was talking.

"Tyler, I need you to focus. You have to get out of there."

"The doggie has the doll."

"I know. We have to figure out how to get it back from him."

"Do you have any dog biscuits?" I asked.

"No."

"Do you have any chew toys?"

"No."

"What about a tranquilizer dart?"

"Try to make friends with it," Kelley suggested.

I turned my attention to the dog. Though it was a big, scary-looking Rottweiler, it wasn't really growling or anything. It was just lying on the ground with the doll between its front paws. It could probably take the head off the doll in one bite. Actually, it could probably swallow the doll whole. What would happen to me then? Would my real body be sizzled by stomach acids while the doll made its way through the dog's digestive tract?

I supposed there would be a lot of fame associated with being "the kid who was digested by a dog without actually being eaten by the dog." But I'd be dead and unable to enjoy it.

Now the dog growled. It was a long, low growl. My family had never owned dogs, so I wasn't entirely sure how to translate this. My cat's communication was simple: Any noise it made meant either "Feed me" or "I hate you." Though I knew enough about dogs to realize that the growling didn't mean it wanted to be stick-fetching buddies, I didn't know how close it was to biting the doll in half.

I put out my hand. "Hey, boy."

The dog did not stop growling. I wished I had something to toss it as a treat. Unfortunately, I hadn't brought either of my toes.

Dammit! I should've asked Adam to get them for me! They could be sewn back on!

"Who's my precious baby?" I asked. "Who's my lovey lovey wiggle wuggums?" I didn't say this in the standard baby-talk voice, which probably reduced its impact. The dog looked at me as if to say…actually, I have no clue what the dog was thinking. Nothing good, I assume.

"Do you need me to climb over and help?" Kelley asked.

The fact that she hadn't already climbed over the fence to help made it clear that she didn't really want to do it. I didn't blame her. At this point, I wouldn't blame her if she lassoed me with a steak necklace and fed me to that beast.

"No, it's cool," I said. "I've got this covered." I crouched down, putting myself at eye level with the ferocious monster. "What's your name, buddy?"

There was a name tag on his collar, so I crept forward a couple of feet, v-e-r-y slowly, to get a better look.

The dog's name was Tyler.

"Hey, we've got the same name," I said. I gave the dog a great big friendly smile to show him that we were awesome friends and I meant him no harm. "That's pretty cool, don't you think?"

I'm not sure why I thought Tyler the Dog would give a crap that we had the same name. His growling continued. My hands were sweating like a zookeeper in a sauna (or, I guess, anybody in a sauna—I don't know why I singled out zookeepers), so I wiped them off on my jeans and then crawled forward a bit more.

The growling definitely got louder.

"Maybe you should just leave it," said Kelley.

Not a chance. If I was going to go after gun-toting thugs to get the doll back, I sure wasn't going to leave it in the jaws of a ginormous dog. One of our neighbors had a dog, and I'd occasionally seen the white cotton innards of its stuffed toys scattered throughout the yard…and that was a wiener dog. If I didn't get the voodoo doll back, I had no doubt that Tyler would shred it down to the individual threads.

I crept a bit closer.

The growling got even louder.

I crept back a bit.

The growling didn't get quieter.

"You know, Tyler, we're alike in more ways than just our name," I said to the dog, not quite sure where I was going with this yet. I thought about it for a second. Nope, nowhere to go with that line of logic, so I switched gears. "If you give me back the doll, I will find you the biggest, juiciest strip of bacon that has ever been gouged out of a pig, and we'll—"

"What do you think you're doing?" asked a gruff voice behind me.

What *was* I doing exactly? Having an English-language conversation with a dog in an effort to persuade him to give me back a doll. It's probably good that I was interrupted.

I glanced over my shoulder. It was an old man in a brown

jumpsuit with lots of grease spots on it. He wasn't pointing a shotgun at me, but from the looks of him, I suspected that he had shotguns hidden all over this place for easy access.

"Your dog has my doll," I said.

"That's not what I asked."

"That's kind of what you asked, isn't it?"

"No."

"Okay, maybe not. Your dog has my doll, so I'm trying to get it back."

"You need to move along. You're not welcome here, you thieving bastard."

"I'm not thieving anything! I'm trying to get back what your dog thieved. Stole. What your dog stole."

"If you don't want to lose a hand, you'd best be going."

I stood up.

"Please, sir, I'm not trying to cause any problems. All I want is my doll back."

"You punks are always throwing stuff at my dog. He's a good dog. Never hurts nobody who's pure of heart."

"I didn't throw anything at him. He knocked me over and took it!"

"Well, that's your side of the story."

I stood up as straight as I could, which was kind of difficult because my foot was really starting to hurt again. I hadn't quite noticed that it had gone numb. Maybe I couldn't negotiate with a canine, but I was *not* leaving this junkyard until I got my doll back.

"Sir, you have stolen property. You can give me back the doll, or I can come back here with my dad's lawyer. Do you really want that?"

The old man spat out a small brown blob of something nasty. "I ain't scared of lawyers. My nephew's a lawyer. I think he'll give your poppa's lawyer a run for his money."

"Are you kidding me? It's just a stupid doll! What are you going to do? Play make-believe with it?"

The old man whistled, and Tyler (the dog version) bounded over to him, the doll still in its mouth. The old man took the doll from him and wiped off some slobber.

"Grandpa?"

"Now I told you to wait inside," said the old man to the little girl who'd also come out of the structure. She looked about six years old, and she had golden curls and big eyes and wore a simple pink dress.

"I know, Grandpa," said the little girl. "I just got scared." She lowered her eyes. "I get scared a lot now that Mom and Dad passed on."

"I know, Gertie, I know," said the old man, "It's hard. Is there any way I can make you feel better?"

She wiped a tear from her eye and then looked up. "I sure would like that new doll you've got."

The old man nodded. "Well, Gertie, I don't know anybody who would be coldhearted enough to refuse a doll to a precious little girl."

"Right here," I said, waving a hand in the air. "You don't want that doll. That doll is garbage. It's gross."

"It's the most beautiful doll I've ever seen," said Gertie.

"That doll is crap," I said. Was six years old too young to hear the word crap? "I mean crud," I corrected. "And it's not mine. It belongs to a little girl on a farm who looks a lot like you."

"I'd give anything to live on a farm," said Gertie. "She's so lucky. I bet she has hundreds of dolls."

I looked over to Kelley for assistance. She was staring through the fence at the unfolding events as if unable to believe what she was witnessing.

The little girl's eyes widened. "Oh! Your foot is bleeding! Grandpa, we need to call a doctor!"

"We're not calling anybody but the cleanup crew to gather his scattered remains if he doesn't get out of here," said the old man.

As if on cue, Tyler the Dog let out a threatening bark and then growled some more, keeping his mouth open enough to reveal what looked like about six thousand sharp teeth.

"I'm not leaving without the doll," I said.

"You don't have a choice in this matter," the old man told me. "You are trespassing on private property, and the doll now belongs to my granddaughter. I don't know what's so special about this doll that you would deprive a dying little girl of the joy she would receive from it, but it's time to let it go. Walk on out of here."

He handed the doll to the little girl, who beamed and hugged it to her chest.

What was I supposed to do? Tackle the little girl? Let out a battle cry and wrestle her to the ground? I guessed that the doll was about as safe as it had been since the car had gotten stolen, but still, to be this close to getting it back...

What would happen if I *did* tackle her?

Tackling a terminally ill six-year-old girl with deceased parents, angelic features, and golden curls was probably not good for one's karma, but I didn't believe in karma, so...

No.

No, no, no.

No, no, no, no, no, no, no, no, no, no, no, no, no, no.

No.

Of course, I didn't *have* to tackle her. I could just grab it out of her hand. Yeah, she might cry, but I'd cry if I lost any more toes, and which would be more pathetic?

I tensed up, ready to do what needed to be done.

"Ew, it's covered in dog spit!" said Gertie, tossing the doll back to the Rottweiler. It caught the doll in the air and shook it, and as the world began to spin again, I flopped back onto the ground.

I realize this chapter is running a little long, but I don't want to use that as the cliffhanger. It's too close to what's already happened, and I don't quite trust that it will keep you reading to the next chapter, not with so many other entertainment options available to you.

As the blur became shapes and then objects with color and then something that passed for the real world that wasn't being very nice to me lately, I realized that I was moving. Not gracefully, but I was on my feet, doing sort of a zombie-like stagger as Kelley held my hand and tried to keep me upright. We were no longer in the junkyard, but we were, unfortunately, still in the dangerous part of town that contained the junkyard.

"Watch your feet," said Kelley. "Uneven sidewalk."

I looked down at my feet and wished I hadn't. I really needed some shoes. All of this blood was truly horrific and unfair to the people around me who had to look at it.

But hey, I was still conscious. Still fighting to stay alive. I'm not saying that I'm a Greek god or anything, but you've got to admit that my bravery was pretty impressive. I mean, sure, James Franco cut off his own arm in *127 Hours*, but that was a movie, and this is real life. And I mean, sure, the movie was based on a true story, and I'm not trying to say that losing a couple of toes is as traumatic as cutting off your arm to free yourself from being pinned underneath a boulder, but...give me my moment, okay?

It really is past time to wrap up this chapter, so I'm going to do the best I can with the whole cliffhanger thing, and I hope you'll stick with me.

"Do you have to go to the bathroom?" I asked Kelley.

CHAPTER 14

"No," Kelley replied.

"Okay," I said.

I noticed that Kelley was holding the doll. The doll! She had it! Right there! In her hand! Holding it! Yes!

"You've got the doll," I told her.

"I know."

"You're the best girlfriend ever."

"I know."

"Will you marry me?" I asked.

"Not right now."

There was a cab parked at the end of the block. The same cab as before? As we got closer, I could see the driver, and, yes! It was! The same cab! Right there! Waiting for us! Saved! Saved! Saved!

Adam was seated in the front. He kind of looked permanently traumatized, but I couldn't see well enough to be sure.

Kelley and I got into the backseat. I hoped the cabdriver didn't try to add a surcharge for bloodstains.

The driver turned around. He looked exhausted. "Got any Red Bull?" he asked.

"Not on me."

"Bummer." He looked sad.

The cab pulled away from the curb. My vision was finally clear, and my brain was less foggy, and it seemed like the right time to ask millions of questions.

"What happened?" I asked.

"I got the doll back," Kelley said.

"Thank you. How'd you do it?"

"I asked nicely."

"No, really, how'd you do it?"

"I screamed and climbed over the fence. Then I told him that since his junkyard was connected by a secret passageway to a chop shop, he probably didn't want me to have to call the police."

"Good thinking."

"It didn't work. But I told him that there were a bunch of shot-up, dead criminals in the chop shop and somebody might think he was involved. That worked."

"Then you carried me over the fence?"

"Do you *think* I carried you over the fence?"

"I guess not."

"He opened the gate and let us out."

"That was nice of him."

"He wasn't that nice about it."

I leaned forward. "Hey, Adam, how are you holding up?"

"I'm not. Please don't ask anymore."

"So where are we headed?"

"While you were off getting mutilated, I was able to make some calls," Kelley said.

"With my phone," said the cabdriver, apparently wanting to make sure he got credit for his role in solving our problems, if I were to ever write a book about them.

"The lady at Esmeralda's House of Jewelry said that she'd be happy to take a look at the doll and that she'd stay open late for us."

"Sweet!"

"I called your mom and assured her again that you weren't dead."

"Thank you."

"She sounded mad."

"I'm sure she is."

"And that's without me telling her about the car. You get to do that."

"Joy."

I wondered how much trouble I'd be in, if any. If this situation were an algebra equation, variable A would be the dismantling of my mom's car. Variable B = Disobeying her by not coming home when told to do so. Variable C = Letting too much time pass between reassurances that I wasn't dead. However, variable D = Gory foot injury, which would gain me sympathy points. Variable E = Relief that I wasn't dead. Variable F = Carjacking victim. I wasn't driving where I was supposed to, but the actual theft of the car wasn't my fault. Variable G = Car was not actually damaged, just taken apart. Maybe there was some blood on the paint, but when she got the car back, it would still be in perfectly decent shape.

Actually, the car might have taken a bullet hit or two. Variable G probably had to be removed from the equation if I wanted to be mathematically accurate.

In terms of getting in trouble, SUM (A + B + C) < SUM (D + E + F), so I'd be fine.

If you really stopped to analyze things and ignored elements like Ribeye still being alive and possibly vengeful, and lots of questions I'd have to answer from the police, and no guarantee that the doll could be stripped of its power, and possible infection that could cause me to lose my entire leg, and terrifying night-mares for the rest of my natural life, and unresolved guilt about the death of Mr. Click, and the possibility that our replacement history teacher could be even meaner...things were delightful.

I noticed that the cab's fare meter was getting close to triple digits. None of us had credit cards, and I didn't think we had a hundred dollars between us. That didn't even count a tip. I was pretty sure this guy would want a tip.

"Well," I said, trying to think of something to say that would lighten the mood, "we've sure had an...ummm...wacky night."

Kelley glared at me. "Wacky?"

"Parts of it were wacky." I forced a smile.

"Don't try to lighten the mood."

"Sorry."

"Sometimes it's okay for the mood to be grim."

"Gotcha."

A tear trickled down Kelley's cheek. She wiped it away.

"Do you want to know what happened to my foot?" I asked.

"You told me."

"When?"

"After we walked through the gate."

"Oh. What did I say?"

"You said the carjackers used the pin on the doll."

"Yep. My toes flew right off." I swooped my hand in the air to demonstrate how they'd flown off. I wasn't doing so well with the advice about it being okay to be grim. I guess I've just never been particularly mopey.

"Are you sure they didn't do it with...I don't know, pliers or something?" It was kind of cute how Kelley was clinging to that last shred of nonbelief in the supernatural.

"No. It was the doll. Do you think you could love somebody with only eight toes?"

She gave me a really funny look, and that's when I realized that we had never said "I love you."

Was now the time? Weren't people supposed to express their true love at stressful moments when one of them was injured? What if the doll got poked again and my head flew off without me ever getting to tell Kelley how I truly felt?

Maybe this wasn't a good moment. Maybe this was the worst possible moment. Maybe only a rock-stupid, nose-picking, drooling, "Duuuuhhhh!"-saying imbecile could think this was an appropriate moment for matters of romance.

I wished my life came with a musical soundtrack to help me figure out how to behave. Maybe the hit single "Love Theme from *A Bad Day for Voodoo*" was playing right now. What if with a single kiss the entire world and its problems could disappear, if only for a moment?

Well, okay, the entire world had sort of vanished during my dizzy spells, and it wasn't such a great feeling. But this would be different.

It's a bad day (bad day) for voodoo.
Girl, you know I'm right.
A bad day (bad day) for voodoo.
Even though I guess it's night.
I've gotta go for a kiss.
Somethin' I just can't miss.
'Cause we could be in bliss.
So girl please don't diss.
And I hope you don't hiss.
A bad day (bad day) for voodoo.
A bad daaaaaaayyyyyyyy for
   voo-hoo-hoo-hoo-doooo-ee-oo.

I started to lean in for a kiss.

Horror movie music began to play on my soundtrack.

I realized that this was *not* going to be one of those cinema moments where the hero and heroine suddenly start passionately kissing. I quickly reversed gears before Kelley noticed my bad timing.

"I'm sorry about your foot," said Adam. "I never meant for anything like that to happen."

"It's okay."

"No, it's not. Friends don't do things like that."

"Really, don't worry about it."

"I'm going to make it up to you," Adam promised. "I don't care how long it takes. Maybe...I don't know, maybe there's a lab that's developed a brand-new line of artificial toes, toes that they're still experimenting with, ones with retractable toenails or something like that, maybe really strong toes where you could hang upside down with just one of them—don't monkeys have those long toes where they can dangle? I'll figure out a way to get you on the list. And if you don't want that, if you want plastic toes that don't do anything special, I'll make that happen too. Whatever you want. And you will never do homework again. English homework, math homework, chemistry, economics, home ec, PE...I'm doing it all for you. Maybe not PE. I can't do PE for you. But any work you take home, just pass it on to me."

"You don't have to do my homework."

"I do. And I'll do it *right*, not the way I do my own homework. And you can have all of my video games. Maybe the ones you already have you can let me keep so I have something to play, but everything else is yours. Tonight. As soon as we get the doll fixed, I'm going to put them all in a box and bring them over. I swear."

"I don't think we're going to have a lot of free time tonight, even after we fix the doll," I said.

"Well, whenever. Whenever we have some free time. I'm not going to renege on this. Kelley is a witness. And Kelley, you can go into my room and pick three things you want. Any three. I didn't drag you into this, Tyler did, but I'm so sorry for dragging Tyler into this and making him drag you into it."

"I don't want any of your things, but thanks," said Kelley.

"You've never been in my room. I've got lots of stuff. Tell her, Tyler."

"You don't need to give all of your things away," I said. "It's fine, really."

Adam shook his head. "I'm not going to do dumb things anymore. Never again. Those days where I was constantly doing dumb things—they were fine for a while; they've worked for me so far. But they have to end. I can't keep living like this. I can't keep being the friend who messes everything up. I want to be the friend you introduce to other people. I want people to say, 'This is Adam, and he is my friend,' instead of, 'This is Adam, he's a little better when you get to know him, but not much.' I want you to be proud of me. You too, Kelley, even though I know that'll never happen. You guys are going to see a brand-new Adam Westell. I may not even keep the name Adam. Maybe I'll be Blake. Or Ziggy. Or I'll make up a name that nobody has ever had. Something without vowels. Zgmf. Or something that isn't pronounced the way it's spelled. Didn't some guy do that one time? I don't remember. But I promise you, both of you, that I'm not going to be the one who ruins everything anymore. I'm going to be the one who solves problems, not causes them. I'm going to be the one you can count on, the one you call when you need help, not the reason you call somebody else. As soon as I saw all of that blood on you, I knew—"

"What blood?" asked the cabdriver.

"Uh," said Adam.

The driver applied the brakes and turned around to stare at me. "If you're bleeding inside my vehicle, I'm gonna cut you."

"Wouldn't that make the problem worse?"

Hadn't Kelley, Adam, and I been discussing my injuries right here in the cab where he could hear us? Maybe the driver was a polite individual who made it a point not to eavesdrop on other people's conversations, and so he'd been thinking of a favorite song or something while we discussed my missing toes. Or maybe he was moderately stupid. Either way, he looked pretty darn mad.

"I'm gonna kick you out and then cut you. Where are you bleeding?"

"Nowhere."

"Don't lie to me." He pulled off to the side of the road and shut off the engine. "I just had my cab cleaned after this lady gave birth in it a couple days ago, and I'm not going through that again. You kids can just pay me and get out." He tapped the meter. "That's one-oh-three."

As has been previously mentioned, we didn't have much money. If you choose to take life lessons from this book, and I hope you don't, one of them would be that at some point, the cabdriver is going to want to be paid, and if you knew you didn't have enough cash, you should have figured something out along the way instead of simply hoping that the problem would disappear.

Kelley, Adam, and I all did that thing where you look at each other with "So, do *you* have any money?" expressions even though you already know the answer. Like when your dad looks in the pantry and says, "Who ate all of the Ho Hos?" and you and your friends all look at each other, even though all of you were there for the Ho Ho–eating party.

"We're not sleazeballs," I assured him. "I promise you'll get your money."

"Good. Then hand it over."

"We don't have it right...y'know...*now*."

The driver narrowed his eyes. "Define 'now.'"

"On us."

"You let me drive you all this way and you didn't have money for the fare?"

"We never thought we'd need you this long. We actually didn't think we'd need a cab at all. But my car got stolen, and we needed somebody to do a high-speed chase, and...well, you remember, you were there. We were never going to jump out and run. My parents will pay you. I guarantee it."

"And are your parents in the cab with you right now?"

"Uh, no."

"Then we have a problem, don't we?"

"No, no, no, there's no problem. You'll get your money. If you have to drop us all the way back off at my house, that's fine. I'll make sure you get paid."

The driver sighed. "You seem like good kids. Well, no, you seem like rotten kids, but you don't seem like thieves." He reached into his pocket and handed me a business card. "This is how you get in touch with me. I expect you to do so. Understand?"

"Yes, sir."

We all sat there for a moment.

"Are you making us get out?" I asked.

"Yes, I am."

"Is there any chance you could take us to the jewelry shop? I mean, we've promised to pay you, so what's another ten bucks on the fare, right?"

The driver opened his door and got out of the cab. Kelley and

Adam hurriedly got out as well. The driver opened my door, saw my foot, and then gave me one of the ugliest scowls I'd ever seen.

"There's…there's…I didn't know you were bleeding *that* much! I thought you scraped up your elbow or something! Look at that!"

"It's not leaking that bad," I insisted. "See? There's barely any on the floor."

"That's worse than the umbilical cord stain! Get out! Now!"

The driver grabbed me by the shirt collar and pulled me out of the car. He raised his fist.

"I'm not a violent person except in the monster truck audience," he said, "but this is a bunch of garbage. You think you can just bleed all over my cab and not suffer the consequences?"

"I didn't bleed all over it!" I said. "It was only a little bit! There was no spurting!"

"It's spurting right now!"

I looked down at my foot. "That's not spurting. That's dripping."

"It's dripping a lot."

"That's because you pulled me out of the car. It wasn't dripping that much inside. I'll clean it up. I promise. Get me some hot water and a sponge, and I'll clean it up right now."

He slammed me against the car. Kelley let out a quick scream. "It would be different if you wanted me to take you to the hospital," said the driver. "That I could get behind. But you, you're being inconsiderate with your blood while you're making me take you to a jewelry store! I should call the cops."

"I'm okay with that right now," I said.

The cabdriver glanced at something behind me. I glanced

over there too. Somebody was on the other side of the street a few blocks away, running toward us. He was wearing a white dress. Or a hospital gown.

"You're not even worth it," the driver said. "I want my fare before the end of the night."

"You'll get it."

"Give me some collateral. Give me your driver's license so I know how to get in touch with you."

I nodded, quickly took out my wallet, and handed him my license. It had the worst picture ever taken of any human being in the entire history of mankind, but for once, I didn't care about the shame of showing it to somebody.

The driver shoved the license into his pocket. "I need more," he said. "Give me that doll that you're so obsessed with so I know you'll pay me."

I shook my head. "I can't do that."

He slammed me against the side of the cab again.

Adam let out a battle cry and ran at the driver. I've gotta be honest with you, Adam is not somebody who intimidates me, but it was one hell of a battle cry, and I was glad he wasn't running at me.

The driver...he didn't actually punch him. He sort of did this move where he grabbed Adam's arm and swung him around, almost like a square dance. Adam kept running for another ten feet or so and then tumbled to the ground. The intimidation inspired by his battle cry disappeared.

Kelley ran at him.

The driver yanked the doll out of my hand. "Stop!" he shouted at her.

Kelley stopped.

"I am *not* going to hit a girl, but I *will* poke this doll's eye out! I don't know exactly what's going on here, but I do know that you don't want this doll's eye to get poked out!"

The man was still running toward us. It was definitely a hospital gown. He was about two blocks away.

The driver shoved me to the ground and got back in his cab. He started the engine while Kelley helped me back up.

"Tyler?" said Adam.

I threw open the back door to the cab, but it sped off. I chased after it for a couple of steps, landed on my foot wrong, and fell back onto the pavement.

"Tyler!" Adam's voice was filled with terror.

"What?"

"*Look!*" he shouted, pointing at the man running toward us.

I looked over there. It was Mr. Click.

CHAPTER 15

During the day's events, there had been several different moments where the proper reaction was to freak out. We freaked out way more at this than we had the others.

Mr. Click was wearing a hospital gown. His head was tilted to the side at kind of a weird angle. His mouth was wide open, though he wasn't making any noise.

If you're good at catching continuity errors, my guess is that right now you're thinking, "Wait a minute. Mr. Click was missing his left leg, so how can he run?" That's exactly what I was thinking too, although you're probably being calmly inquisitive while I was thinking, *His leg! His leg! His leg's back on! His leg's back on!*

Actually, though I don't remember it word for word, I'm pretty sure the thoughts running through my head were:

Aaah! Zombie Click!

His leg! His leg!

I'm gonna die!

Zombie Click!

His leg's back on! His leg's back on!

Aaah!

The cabdriver stole my—Zombie Click!!—doll and—Zombie Click!!!—what if he—Zombie Click!!!—damages it—Zombie Click!!!

His left leg was back on, but it was all purple.

Clearly, what we had here was a situation where Mr. Click had returned from the dead to seek vengeance against those who had killed him. I couldn't blame him—I mean, I would've done the same. I only wished that he could've timed his undead revenge for when we were still in the cab and could have driven away really fast.

Mr. Click stretched out his arms and opened his mouth even wider, though he remained silent.

He didn't go for me. He went for Adam.

He pounced on top of him, clamping his hands around Adam's neck as if to strangle him. The cab turned the corner and disappeared from sight, but that problem was much less important than the risk of Adam's brains being eaten, so I grabbed the back of Mr. Click's gown and tried to pull him away.

The gown tore.

This was officially the worst day ever.

Adam let out a high-pitched shriek that did not shatter every piece of glass in a six-block radius but sounded like it should have. Kelley and I each grabbed one of Mr. Click's arms and tried to pull him away. The arm I was holding twisted and made a grotesque *snap* sound at the shoulder.

Adam frantically scooted away, now screaming as silently as Mr. Click. My ex-history teacher's arm popped out of my grasp and flopped around at his side while Kelley desperately tried to hold on.

I grabbed the same arm, and we both yanked back. There was

another hideous snap, and Mr. Click fell onto the ground, mouth opening and closing like he was trying to bite.

Kelley, Adam, and I packed a lot of screaming into the next few seconds.

"Don't let him eat me!" Adam wailed.

A car pulled onto the street but suddenly sped up, clearly not wanting to get involved.

Mr. Click sat up and then pounced at Adam again. His arms weren't working right, but he kept jerking his shoulders, as if trying to swing his arms around Adam's neck.

I wrapped my arms around Mr. Click's waist and dragged him backward, just a few inches. I couldn't believe how strong he was. When imagining fighting a zombie (and I'm embarrassed to say that I had many times), I always thought I'd be able to overpower them without much difficulty.

"Mr. Click, can you hear me?" asked Kelley. "Can you understand what I'm saying?" I understood what she was trying to do, though because Mr. Click had very little humanity when he was alive, I doubted she'd be able to unlock it when he was dead.

Mr. Click continued to struggle to get at Adam.

"Run!" I shouted at Adam. He seemed to think that was a fine idea and sprinted off.

Mr. Click pulled away from me again, but I jumped on his back, keeping him on the ground. Was he trying to kill Adam or give him one last pop quiz?

"Kick him in the head!" I told Kelley.

She hesitated. She was, after all, a straight-A student who never entertained fantasies about kicking her teachers in the head.

"Do it!"

"What if he can be fixed?"

"*What?*"

"What if he can be fixed, but kicking him in the head messes him up beyond the fixing point?"

"He can't be fixed! Kick him!"

Kelley kicked him in the head. It was a spectacular kick, a goal-scoring kick, and I think it left a dent. But it didn't lower his energy level.

Mr. Click pulled free of me yet again, got to his feet, and took off running after Adam. Though Adam had had a solid head start, he was a pretty lousy runner, so I shouted, "Hurry!" after him.

I started to chase after Mr. Click, but you can guess how well that went, and I stopped after a few steps. Mr. Click raced after Adam, rapidly closing the distance between them until only about ten feet remained…and then his leg popped off again.

It wasn't nearly as gory this time, which is not to say that it was dry. Some red goo stretched from the stump to his leg as he toppled forward, and then he continued to crawl. Although with only one leg and two messed-up arms, he couldn't move very well.

Adam glanced back over his shoulder and seemed to realize that Mr. Click didn't pose as much of a problem anymore. He jogged back to us, giving the zombie a wide berth.

"Are you guys okay?" Adam asked.

"Not so much," I said.

"What just happened?"

"I don't know."

"How did he come back to life?"

"I don't know."

"How did he get out of the morgue?"

"I don't know."

"How did he find us?"

"I don't know."

"Why was he after me?"

"Why *wouldn't* he be after you?" I asked. "You're the one who bought the doll in the first place! You're exactly the person he should be after!"

"Still…"

"No 'still.' Nothing else about this makes sense, but that part does."

Mr. Click was crawling toward us, making poor time.

"Did you know this was going to happen?" Kelley demanded.

"No," Adam insisted.

"Are you sure?"

"If I knew he was going to come back to try to kill me, don't you think I would've been more nervous the rest of the evening?"

"Why do you think this happened?" Kelley asked.

There was a fraction of a second of hesitation before Adam said, "Dunno."

"Are you keeping something from us?" I asked.

Adam shook his head.

"Are you sure?"

"I swear."

"This isn't a good time for secrets."

"I don't have any secrets."

"I'm serious."

"I know."

"You just gave that big speech."

"I still believe in that speech."

"If you have anything to say, say it."

"I don't have anything to say."

"We won't get mad." (I was lying when I said that.)

"I really don't know what happened."

"No clue?"

"None."

"No guesses?"

"None. I mean, it was something with voodoo, I assume."

"I think you know something."

"I don't."

"Tell me."

"I don't know anything."

"I'm not going to stop bugging you."

"Then we're just wasting time."

"So we waste time."

"Don't forget that the cabdriver has the doll."

"Dammit!"

"It'll be okay," Adam assured me. "The doll has to be safe, or you'd be dead, right?"

I ignored that comment. "I've got his card. We'll find a pay phone and call him. Maybe since he's had a few minutes to chill out, he'll be in a more understanding mood."

I had to stay calm and think positive. Ultimately, what was the driver going to do with the doll? He wasn't going to take a hacksaw to it or anything like that. There would probably be some blackmail involved, but that was okay. At this point, I was fine with a little light blackmail.

"What do we do with him?" asked Kelley, pointing to Mr. Click.

"Do we need to do anything with him?" Adam asked. "Let's just go."

"We can't leave a zombie on the street."

"Why not?"

"He's dangerous."

"Like that? Who's he gonna outrun?"

"What if somebody sees what they think is a poor, injured man flailing around on the ground and go over to help?"

"Right. Because this place has been swarming with Good Samaritans so far. It's unbelievable how many people ran over to help us with our carjacking problem. People had to take a number. I wish we'd had those flashing signal things you get at busy restaurants that let you know when your table is ready—it was a shame that people had to stand around waiting their turn to help us when they could've been window shopping!"

"I don't appreciate your tone," said Kelley, "but I'll admit that was kind of clever."

"Thank you."

"But we obviously can't just leave him crawling around in the street."

"Should we put a 'Warning: Zombie' sign around his neck?" Adam asked.

"Stop being clever now."

"If we had a car, we could hide him in the trunk," I said. It was kind of a dumb thing to say, because we did not have a car, and if we'd had a car, it would have saved us all of our problems from the carjacking forward. Unfortunately, sometimes your mouth opens and words come out and they aren't the greatest words in the world and there's nothing you can do about it except hope to do better the next time you talk.

Kelley rolled her eyes. "If we had a car, we never—"

"I withdraw my comment."

"What if we chopped off his head?" Adam asked.

"We're not chopping off his head!" I said.

"Do you have a better idea?"

"Yes. My dumb comment about us having a car was a better idea."

"He can't hurt any innocent pedestrians without a head."

"Didn't this whole thing start because you were scared that we'd go to jail for using the doll on him?" I asked. "We had a zero percent chance of actually getting caught for that."

"Not zero," said Adam.

"Zero point two."

"Zero point six or seven at least."

"Fine. But we at least agree that we probably weren't going to jail for it, right?"

Adam shrugged.

"So if you were worried about getting caught for the voodoo doll, why in the world would you think there wouldn't be a problem with dismembering him?"

"I didn't say dismember. I said decapitate."

"Same thing."

"Well, sure, if you think that chopping off somebody's arms, legs, and head is the same as just chopping off their head."

"You're missing the point."

"My point is that you're accusing me of wanting to dismember an innocent man when I only wanted to decapitate him."

"Well, we're not doing either of them."

"I bet if Kelley said we should chop his head off, we'd do it."

"I am absolutely not suggesting that we chop his head off," said Kelley.

"But if you did…"

"Enough!" I shouted. "All we're going to do is put him someplace where he won't hurt anybody. Any ideas?"

"Let's just drag him to the back of an alley," said Adam.

Kelley shook her head. "I don't want to go into those alleys even without a zombie teacher."

I looked around. "This is a little disrespectful," I admitted, "but what about the sewer?"

"You mean flush him down the toilet?" Adam asked. "You get all whiny because I want to cut his head off, and now you're suggesting we cut him into toilet-sized pieces?"

"Adam, think about what you're saying."

Adam was silent for a moment. "Okay, maybe I didn't understand your plan."

"We lift a manhole cover and throw him down. He won't be able to hurt anybody down there, and if we need him, we'll know where to find him. The worst thing that can happen is that rats chew on him."

"You say 'worst thing' as if being eaten by rats wasn't actually the worst possible thing that could happen to somebody," said Kelley, cringing.

"He's a zombie. He won't care," I said.

"We don't even know that he's a zombie. He could be possessed."

"I'm pretty sure he's a zombie."

"Either way, I'm not convinced that he can't be fixed. If this happened to you, wouldn't you want people to make sure that rats didn't gnaw on your body? You're all panicked about your foot, but he could wake up without a nose!"

"For the record, I'd like to say that I've been very easygoing about my toes," I said. "I could be doing nothing but bawling and going 'Wahh! My poor toes!' but I've hardly mentioned them at all. So I'd like an apology."

"I didn't say that you were being a baby about them. I said you were panicked. And I'm saying that having your nose gnawed off by sewer rats is worse than losing two of your little toes."

"I'm not sure I agree with…" I considered the two options. "Okay, the rat nose thing is worse. But still, we don't have much choice. It's either drop him in the sewer or drag him into an alley. And we don't know how long we'll have to leave him, so he might have time to crawl out of the alley and kill an old lady."

Kelley sighed. "Okay. Sewer then."

INTERMISSION

Take a break and read *The Hunger Games* again.

CHAPTER 16

"So what if we let the air out of his tires, and then we rig the car so it crushes his arms when he goes to check? He can't give you another F if he doesn't have arms."

"Seems extreme," I said.

"Well…maybe his arms don't actually have to come *off*. We could just make it so they don't work anymore."

Here's the thing about Adam: I knew he was only kidding, but a small part of me suspected that he really would help me rig Mr. Click's car to crush his arms if I asked. Does it make me look bad to admit that my best friend might be a tiny bit psychotic? I hope not.

Whoa. Why did the first chapter suddenly show up? That wasn't supposed to happen. Must have been a software glitch. Sorry about the technical difficulties…I guess that intermission threw everybody off a little bit. We've got it sorted out now, though, and here's the real Chapter 16.

In the movies, manhole covers look like they weigh about three ounces and are made out of Styrofoam. In real life, they weigh about 82,319 pounds and are made out of lead. Though the three of us finally lifted it out of the way, it was a semi-pathetic display of muscular power.

A couple of cars drove by, but they didn't seem concerned with either the three hooligans moving a manhole cover or the one-legged man in a hospital gown crawling around on the road. (Both vehicles were polite enough to steer around him, although their concern may have been the cleanliness of their automobiles.)

"Should I keep watch while you guys drag him?" Adam asked, in a tone of voice that implied that he thought he was being very helpful and selfless.

"No, you can help us drag."

"What if somebody sees us?"

"We'll all keep a lookout while we drag."

"I think it's a mistake."

"Kelley can keep watch then."

"Zombie Click wasn't trying to eat Kelley."

"He wasn't trying to eat you either. He was just opening and closing his mouth. You take his leg. Kelley and I will take his arms."

We dragged him over to the manhole and dropped him in. He landed with a splash and a thud.

That's it. No wacky hijinks. He didn't get wedged in the manhole or stuck on the ladder or land on his head or anything like that, and the cops didn't show up at the exact wrong time, and he wasn't immediately swarmed by thousands of rats and skeletonized. It pretty much worked out just the way we planned.

Alternate but made-up version of previous scene for those of you who were disappointed by the lack of conflict:

"Oh my goodness!" Kelley's lungs bulged through her chest from the intensity of her scream. "His skin is splitting open!"

"And beetles are coming out!" Adam shouted in horror.

Millions of beetles spilled out, far more than should have fit into Mr. Click's body. I had no idea where he'd been keeping them.

"They're mutating!" Kelley screamed in horror.

As we watched in horror, the beetles began to sprout extra legs. They sprouted more and more legs until even millipedes didn't have as many legs as these beetles did. The legs kept popping up until the thousands of beetles were nothing but legs. And then the legs began sprouting legs.

"Too many legs! Too many legs!" Adam screamed in horror.

And then I felt a sharp pain between my shoulder blades. I turned around and gaped at Kelley in horror.

"That's right," she said. "I was evil all along."

"And so was I," said Adam. Kelley pulled out her knife, and then Adam stabbed me in the same place. "All these years of friendship were a fiendish lie just to get to this moment."

They both stabbed me a few more times, being very fair and taking turns.

"This bites," I said in horror. Then I died and came back as a ghost with the ability to use a computer to write books.

And now back to the completely true version of the story, for those of you who understand that in real life there aren't always complications when you're shoving a zombie down an open manhole:

I feel like I should apologize, because the actual book isn't as cool as the stuff I made up. I hope you aren't disappointed with the rest of your reading experience.

Anyway, with the Mr. Click problem thoroughly dealt with and certain not to come back to haunt us at any inconvenient moment later in the evening, we turned our attention to the pressing matter of the frickin' voodoo doll having been stolen again.

A brief history lesson: In the olden days, people weren't smart enough to know how to make cell phones. If you were at home, it wasn't any big deal, because you probably had a phone in your house and you could just make the call there. If you were at a friend's house, it was still fine, because he'd probably let you use his phone, unless you were making what was known as a long-distance call. It doesn't make sense to me either, but that's the way it worked.

If you were outdoors or at a mall or something, you had to use a pay phone where you'd insert a dime (later a quarter...now two quarters), and the bulky contraption would let you make your call.

In the digital age, most citizens owned cell phones, making pay phones much less essential. People who owned them used to be able to roll around in their piles of quarters, cackling with glee, but now they could only roll around on a couple of quarters, which made it look more like they were just too lazy to pick the quarters up off the floor before they started rolling around. With pay phones being much less profitable, there was no longer as much need to keep them in working order. So when a quarter would get jammed inside or somebody would have a fight with his girlfriend and smash the receiver against a brick wall or the phone would get struck by lightning or some jerks would say, "Hey, let's do us some vandalism, huh, huh, huh," the phone would not be repaired.

This history lesson became important to me as we walked around trying to find a pay phone that was in working order. They don't exist. By the time we found the third nonworking phone, we were all ready to have individual nervous breakdowns, and it became clear that a different strategy was in order.

"Let's cry," said Adam.

"It's going to be okay," I assured him, even though now I knew that the world was a dark, scary place that hated teenagers.

"It seems like we've been walking too long to still be in the bad part of town," said Adam. "Shouldn't we have reached a highway or something by now?"

"It feels like we've been walking longer than we have because I'm slowing us down," I said, jiggling my bloody foot for emphasis.

"It does seem like we've been walking a long time," Kelley agreed. "I don't know this area, but I don't remember it being this big."

"So what are you saying?" I asked.

"I'm not saying anything," said Adam. "It was only an observation."

"We need to start knocking on doors," said Kelley.

"Do you think that's a good idea?"

"No, Tyler, I suggested it because I think it's a bad idea, and I wanted to make sure we continued with today's trend."

"Are you being sarcastic?"

"Do you think I'm being sarcastic?"

"I don't know. I really don't know."

"We can't fight amongst ourselves," said Adam. "That's what it wants."

"That's what what wants?"

"I'm not sure. But don't you sense that? I can't quite describe it, but don't you have the feeling that something's just a little bit off?"

"Well, yeah, once Mr. Click's leg shot across the classroom, I started to think that the universe might have gone a bit askew."

"See, more sarcasm. It wants us to be sarcastic. Snark is its weapon."

"You're an idiot," I told him.

"That's not snark. That's just rude."

"Look, we need to not turn this into something bigger than it is. We're not wandering around *The Twilight Zone*."

"*Twilight Zone*!" said Adam. "That's what I was trying to think of! Yeah, it's like we're in *The Twilight Zone*! Thank you! That was driving me crazy."

"I'm serious. You need to stop getting carried away," I said. "We're still in the real world, except that voodoo exists. Everything else is normal."

"Look!" Adam said, pointing ahead. "That pay phone is the exact same one we just passed! We're in a loop!"

The three of us walked over to the phone. "No, it's not," said

Kelley. "The other one had different graffiti, and the nine key was missing. This one doesn't look anything like it."

Adam studied the phone, then nodded. "Yeah, you're right. Also, this one doesn't have a cord."

We each cursed in turn and then resumed walking.

"I think we're getting close to some houses," Kelley said. "Somebody is going to be nice and let us use their phone."

"What if we knock on the door of a meth lab?" asked Adam.

"As long as it's a meth lab with a phone, I don't care."

"I care," I said. "Let's skip the meth lab if possible."

The neighborhood was well lit, and none of the homes looked as if they were dangerous hotbeds of illegal activity. A middle-aged man was walking his Schnauzer at the far end of the block, but he turned around when he noticed us.

At the closest corner was a one-story white home with a white truck in the driveway. The lawn needed mowing, but not in a the-owner-was-murdered-weeks-ago-and-nobody-is-maintaining-the-yard sort of way.

"What approach should we take?" I asked.

"No special approach," said Kelley. "We just say that you've been hurt and ask if we can use their phone."

"What if they say no but they'll call an ambulance for us?"

"I don't know. We'll just play it by ear." Kelley paused and massaged her scalp, as if she had a skull-crushing headache. "Sorry, I forgot who I'm with. Playing it by ear is a terrible idea. Okay, if they say no but offer to call 911 for us…we pretty much have to let them, right? Otherwise it would look too suspicious."

"Yeah, I guess so." We walked up to the front porch, but I

didn't go up the two steps with Kelley and Adam. "I'll wait here so I don't track blood on the porch," I said.

Kelley rang the doorbell.

Inside, a dog barked.

The peephole went dark for a moment, and then the door opened a couple of inches, as far as the inside chain lock would go. A heavyset man in a white T-shirt narrowed his eyes at us.

"Unless you're selling Girl Scout cookies, I'm not buying anything."

"We're not soliciting," said Kelley. She gestured at me. "My boyfriend lost a couple of toes. Do you have a phone we could borrow?"

"How'd he lose the toes?"

"Fireworks."

"Serves the little bastard right."

He slammed the door.

"Next house?" I asked.

Kelley shook her head. She rang the doorbell again. The peephole went dark, as if the guy were checking that it was still us on his porch, and then he reopened the door.

"What?"

"We really need a phone."

"Last year, you little crapheads shot those things off until two in the morning. My dog spent eight hours hiding under the bed, and when I finally dragged her out, all of her fur had fallen off."

"I'm sorry to hear that."

"You and your blown-off toes can just bite me. I wish you'd swallowed one."

"We'll ask somebody else."

"And why don't they sell Girl Scout cookies in stores? Why do you take a product that people actually want to buy and put a stranglehold on it like that? Tell you what, you find me a box of Thin frickin' Mints, and you can use my phone to call 1-800 horoscope numbers for all I care."

"Thank you for your time."

"Have you ever seen a Shih Tzu without fur? You can't un-see that. It'll haunt your dreams."

"We're leaving now."

"Know what the Boy Scouts tried to sell me? Tickets to the Scout-O-Rama. Why the hell would I ever want to go to the Scout-O-Rama? Did you bastards mess with my satellite dish? Because I haven't been able to get Showtime on Demand to work all evening."

Kelley and Adam turned and walked off the man's front porch. He slammed the door shut. Without a word, we walked to the next house.

Kelley rang the doorbell. Inside the house, a recorded voice that sounded a lot like Cookie Monster said, "Doorbell! Doorbell!" It was, I have to admit, a pretty cool doorbell ringtone.

The front door opened, revealing an old man with Albert Einstein hair. "May I help you?" he asked.

"Could we borrow your phone?" Kelley asked. She gestured to me. "A car ran over my boyfriend's foot."

"So much blood," said the old man, nodding approvingly. "So much blood."

"Your phone?"

"Tell me, young lady, are you frightened? Right now?"

"A little."

"Because you look like the perfect candidates for my experiment…" He smiled. "…in fear."

CHAPTER 17

"I think we'll try another house," said Kelley.

"All right. I hope your boyfriend's foot gets better."

We walked to the next house. Kelley rang the doorbell. The guy who answered was unshaven and wore a base-ball cap.

"Sorry to disturb you, but could we borrow your phone?" Kelley asked. "My boyfriend was carving lumber, and the saw blade popped loose and cut off his toes."

"Ooooohhhhh no, no, no," said the guy. "I'm not falling for *that* one! Go steal somebody else's phone."

"We're not trying to steal anything."

"Uh-huh. Yeah, right. Like anybody really loses toes."

"It's true," I said, lifting my injured foot.

"Uh-huh. Karo syrup and red food coloring. I may have been born in a barn, but I wasn't born in a barn last week."

"No, really, I'll take off the cloth if you want to see the red spongy part."

"Find another sucker. Not of blood…you know what I mean."

He shut the door. We walked to the next house.

"I should do the talking this time," Adam suggested.

"So, what, you're saying that the mad scientist would have acted normal if you'd been the one talking?" Kelley asked.

"Maybe this neighborhood hates women."

"Are you kidding me?"

"I deserve a chance."

I waved my hand. "I'm the one who's going to bleed out, so I get to decide. Kelley should talk, one hundred percent."

"Why not let me redeem myself?"

"We'll be on the lookout for another way for you to redeem yourself."

"Fine. Whatever. I just hope we find a phone before gangrene sets in."

"Gangrene takes…" I trailed off, because I suddenly realized that I didn't have the slightest idea how long gangrene took to set in. Had we covered gangrene in biology class? What if my foot was already infected? What if I peeled off the cloth and was greeted by the sight of a blackened, shriveled, rotten-apple-looking appendage that was only recognizable as my foot because it was stuck to the end of my leg?

"It takes about forty-eight hours," said Kelley.

"Oh well, I'm glad you studied up on gangrene for tonight," said Adam. "How do we know she's right? Is she a doctor? Is she even a medical student? Why would she even want to know something like that?"

"Excuse me for taking an interest in the world around me and retaining information!" said Kelley. "If you think Tyler has some genetically enhanced super-strain of gangrene, fine, you do the talking."

"No, no, I still vote for you talking," I said. "I trust you on the gangrene. Completely. Just ring the doorbell."

Kelley rang the doorbell. A smiling blonde woman who looked about my mom's age answered. She wore an apron over her light blue dress and an oven mitt.

"Well, hello," she said. She called inside the house. "Glenn! Donna! Franklin! We have guests!"

"Could we borrow your phone?" Kelley asked. "My boyfriend—"

"Of course you can borrow our phone. What a silly thing to ask. What kind of Basers would we be otherwise?"

"Basers?"

"Yes, Basers," said the woman, offering no further explanation. "Oh, where are my manners? I keep losing those silly things, don't I? My name is Mildred. You already know Glenn, Donna, and Franklin."

Three people stepped into the foyer behind her. Glenn (identifiable because he wore a pullover sweater with "Glenn" on the front) had slicked back hair and a wide smile with perfect teeth. I assume he was Mildred's husband, because he put his arm around her waist and pulled her close while she beamed.

Donna and Franklin didn't wear their names on their clothes, but it wasn't difficult to tell who was who. They were both teenagers, probably even sixteen-year-olds like us, and it kind of looked like they were twins. They were good-looking and had much better complexions than any of the three of us. Their teeth were also perfect, although not *too* perfect...I mean, I wasn't ready to scream, "Their teeth! They're unnaturally white!" or anything like that. They simply had nice teeth.

They were both wearing pajamas, which I guess wasn't *too* weird, even though it was only about eight o'clock. I mean, if you're not planning to go anywhere, you might as well be comfy.

Mildred's smile faltered. "It *is* polite to introduce yourself when meeting strangers for the first time," she said.

"Oh, I'm so sorry," said Kelley. "I'm Kelley, with two *e*'s."

"Where are the *e*'s?" Glenn asked.

"One before the two *l*'s, one after the two *l*'s."

Glenn seemed to go over that in his mind. "Ah. Nontraditional spelling, I see."

"It's not that uncommon, but yeah, a lot of people get it wrong."

"I'm Adam," said Adam.

"Adam, eh?" asked Glenn. "I guess we'd better make sure to keep you away from our apples!"

Mildred, Glenn, Donna, and Franklin all laughed.

"But that doesn't mean he can't have some of my delicious homemade apple pie!" said Mildred.

"Oh no, we wouldn't deny anybody that!" said Glenn. "That would be far too cruel!"

"And I'm Tyler," I said, giving them a friendly wave. "I'm the one who's hurt."

"Oh, you poor dear," said Mildred, stepping out of her doorway and looking down at my foot. "That *is* a grotesque injury, isn't it? Well, come on inside, and we'll get you all disinfected."

"I don't want to get blood all over your floor," I said. "If we could borrow your phone, we'll just wait outside."

I noticed that Donna was giving Adam the kind of look that a guy like Adam didn't get from many (also defined as "any") women. This really surprised me, considering the vast chasm between their levels of physical attractiveness. I'm not trying to be superficial, but c'mon, there are societal norms.

"Now don't you worry about our floor," Mildred told me. "Everybody has blood, so I'd be a pretty darn big hypocrite if I judged you for yours. It's not like you're going to go around rubbing your foot against our antique furniture, right?"

"No, that wasn't my plan."

"Well, then it's settled. Come on in, all three of you, and get out of that humidity," said Mildred, beckoning for us to walk into their house. "Franklin, get our guest a towel."

Franklin was giving Kelley the kind of look that she got on a regular basis. Not quite a look that said, *Give me the word and I'll bash your boyfriend over the head with a shovel and then we can slap our tongues together for six or seven hours*, but at least one that said, *Yeah, baby, yeah. You know you want some of this. Sashay that cute body over here and come get yourself a big ol' slice of pure Franklin.*

I did not approve of this look.

This whole family kind of creeped me out, but as long as they had a phone, I wasn't going to run away screaming quite yet. Adam and Kelley walked inside, and by the time I joined them, Franklin had already fetched me a nice, fluffy purple towel.

Mildred crouched down and tied it around my foot. "Don't you worry about staining our towels. We've got more. You just bleed as much as you'd like."

"Thank you."

"We'll get your wound cleaned out in just a tiny short minute.

In the meantime, you three youngsters sit down and relax. Everything will be fine."

We sat down on the soft white couch in their spacious living room. The walls were decorated with religious items, and when I say "decorated," I mean that if you took a digital photograph, there would not be one square pixel of their wall that wasn't covered with something religious.

But it wasn't only one religion. Christianity, Judaism, Hinduism, and countless others were represented, including a bunch that I didn't even recognize. It was like the ultimate religious smorgasbord. There was also a framed picture of "Weird Al" Yankovic, who apparently had a religious cult in his honor.

"I like your décor," I said.

"Does it make you feel comfy?" Mildred asked.

"Yes," I said, even though it made me feel the exact opposite. "Are you interested in religious studies?"

"Oh no. Like I said, we're Basers."

"Basers?"

"Only dead people know what awaits them in the afterlife. Could be heaven or hell, could be reincarnation, could be maggots. If it's maggots, there's really not much we can do, but if it's anything else, intelligent people take advantage of the wide variety of theories and cover their bases. Basers."

I tried to send powerful brain waves in Kelley's direction: *Please don't start a religious debate with this family…please don't start a religious debate with this family…please don't start a religious debate with this family.*

"Sounds like you're being very thorough," said Kelley.

"As thorough as we can be," said Glenn. "It would be a huge bummer to put in all of this time and effort only to find out that the winner was some religion practiced by a tribe of six in Southern Australia."

"A mega-mega bummer," Kelley agreed. "Can we use your phone?"

"Who would you like to call?" asked Mildred.

"A friend to pick us up," I said.

Mildred continued to smile as she shook her head.."Oh no, darling. I don't think so."

"Can Adam come in my room with me and watch TV?" asked Donna.

Adam's eyes widened. He looked suddenly excited, because he didn't get to watch TV with hot girls very often, and also worried, because we all knew that Donna probably wanted to feast upon his beating heart.

Mildred folded her arms in front of her chest. "Now, Donna, what have we discussed about being presumptuous?"

"He's been looking at me the whole time," said Donna with a pout.

"No, I haven't," Adam insisted, stammering a bit. "I've been looking at my friend's bloody foot."

"Liar!" said Donna. "You can't even see the blood through the towel."

"Donna! You mind your manners. You're not too old for the wrench."

"Fine," said Donna. "I didn't want him anyway. He's dog-ugly."

"I don't know what's gotten into you lately," said Glenn, "but this attitude is going to stop in two shakes of a lamb's tail. You apologize to this young man. He is not dog-ugly by any stretch of the imagination. No, he's never going to be on the cover of fashion magazines, but how many people are? He carries off the gawky look better than most people your age. Say you're sorry."

I honestly thought she was going to resort to being a six-year-old and say something like "I'm sorry you're dog-ugly." But she didn't. Her apology was simple ("Sorry") and seemed sincere.

"It's okay," said Adam.

"So can I take him to my room?"

"Not tonight, dear," said Mildred.

"Oh, I don't see that there's anything wrong with them watching some TV," said Glenn. "She did apologize."

Donna hurried over to the couch, grabbed Adam's hand, and pulled him to his feet. "C'mon, let's go!" she said.

"I, uh, shouldn't..." said Adam.

"Adam!" said Kelley.

"I can't," said Adam. "I need to stay with my friend. He's hurt."

"He'll be fine," Donna assured him. "Mom found a squirrel once whose tail had been pulled off, and she cauterized the hole right up."

Adam gave another halfhearted protest, and then Donna quickly led him out of the living room and down a hallway. We heard a door open and then close. Kelley just sat there, her jaw hanging open.

"If Donna gets Adam, then I get Kelley," said Franklin.

"Objection!" I said.

Yeah. That's what I said. "Objection." I'm embarrassed to

even have to type that. Don't *you* wish you had somebody like me to defend your honor?

Glenn chuckled. "Whoa! Did you see him bristle? It was like we had a porcupine in the house." He patted me on the shoulder. "Don't you worry. My boy was only kidding."

"If he touches me, I'm going to claw his eyes out," said Kelley. "Just throwing that out there."

"That was uncalled for," said Mildred. "You're a guest in our home, and you'll abide by our rules. In this household, we do not threaten to claw each other's eyes out. If you want to do that, go someplace else where that kind of rudeness is tolerated."

"Actually, I'd very much like to go someplace else," said Kelley, standing up. "Adam! Get back out here!"

"Sit back down, young lady," said Mildred.

WHAT DO YOU THINK MILDRED SAID NEXT?

A) "Ha ha! Just kidding, you little rapscallions! Here's a free cell phone and a DIY book on how to undo voodoo curses."

B) "I wish I had a free monkey for every time somebody ate a crouton."

C) "I'm sorry, but you're not going anywhere."

D) None of the above.

The answer is C.

CHAPTER 18

"You can't keep us here against our will," I said. Because in a hostage situation, the best thing you can do is inform your captors that they aren't allowed to be doing this.

"We didn't ask for you to disturb us," said Mildred. "We were enjoying a peaceful evening of family time when you came pounding on our door."

Alert readers will remember that we didn't pound on the door. We rang the doorbell. Astute readers will guess that I didn't correct her. I mean, why behave like an Internet troll?

Adam had not yet responded to Kelley's demand that he get back out here. This was a source of concern.

"All we wanted was to borrow your phone," I said. "I was even worried about bleeding in your living room."

The logical way to handle this situation seemed to be to rush for the front door and get the hell out of this house of madness before we could be killed and served as stew. But what about Adam? Was it too late for him? Was his body already in the form of small cubes of meat?

"Just so you know," I said, "all three of us are diseased." (I considered being specific, but the only disease I could think of at that very moment was mad cow, so I decided that the vague approach would be better.) "If you eat us, you'll catch it too."

Mildred laughed. "Why does everybody always assume that we're cannibals?" Then her face fell. "Is it my butt? Does it look big in this dress? Do I look like I've been eating too much?"

"No, your butt looks, uh, charming," I said.

My heart was pounding. I'd had a bunch of guns pointed at me earlier, but that was somehow much less frightening than this creepy, smiley family. I looked at Kelley to see if she was thinking about the same *RUN!!!* plan that I was.

Adam let out a scream.

It wasn't the good kind of scream. It wasn't a scream that sent the message *This is awesome!* or *That really tickles, but I love it!* This was a scream of terror.

That said, I don't want to give the impression that it was a terrified scream that echoed through my brain and would haunt my dreams until the end of my days. There wasn't soul-deep terror in that scream. He just sounded scared. He definitely didn't sound like he was having any fun.

"I love that noise," said Glenn. "Worth every penny of the soundproofing we had to install to avoid alerting the neighbors."

Kelley and I jumped to our feet. My plan was to shove Glenn out of the way, race down the hallway, throw open the door, let Kelley beat up Donna, drag Adam to safety, then let Kelley beat up Mildred while I beat up Franklin. Then we'd try another house.

Much of this plan was designed with the idea that Mildred

would *not* pull out a gun from underneath her apron, so I was very disappointed when she did.

It was only a little gun, but still…

"Sit down," she said.

Adam screamed again.

"I never get tired of that sound," said Glenn.

Mildred probably wouldn't have time to shoot both of us before we rushed her, but a 50 percent survival rate simply wasn't acceptable.

"Our parents will be looking for us," said Kelley.

"I know that, you silly duck," said Mildred. "They usually do."

"They know we're here."

"Yes, I'm sure that before you left the house, you told your mom and dad that you were headed out to go knock on strangers' doors, asking to use their phone."

"They at least know the general area."

"I spy, with my little eye, somebody who is telling a lie. Can anybody guess who that is?"

Nobody answered the question, but we all knew it was Kelley. A couple of small patches of blood had started to seep through the towel.

"I'm gonna start bleeding on your floor," I said, hoping this would provide enough distraction for our daring escape.

"I'm pointing a gun at you," said Mildred. "Believe me, brain matter is a lot harder to get out of the upholstery than blood."

I nodded. Her effort to intimidate me had been successful.

Or had it?

On those crime scene investigation shows, they were always

talking about how you could never truly get rid of blood traces, no matter how hard you tried. Many a criminal had been apprehended because of their false assumptions about the cleaning power of household detergents. But I'd never heard of the lab guys saying, "Oh my, look at this…she forgot to sweep up this chunk of the victim's brain."

So Mildred was bluffing.

She wasn't really going to shoot me.

I was pretty sure she wasn't really going to shoot me.

But she could be lying about her familiarity with brain matter and still be telling the truth about her intent to shoot me.

Obviously, she was trying to sound more threatening than she actually was. Yet if a mob enforcer said, "I've killed thirty-eight people," when he'd only killed twenty-six, you'd still be worried if he took you out on a boat and asked you to hold your feet in a box of cement until it dried.

If she had the gun and the gun was pointed at me, why would she *need* to say something about brain matter? Why did she need to be scarier? I was a sixteen-year-old kid. Was she so worried that I was going to try to rush her and knock the gun away that she made a sinister comment to make sure I stayed in my seat?

Well, to be fair, I *had* considered the idea that she was bluffing, and her comment about the brain matter *had* encouraged me to devote more thought to whether or not that was a good idea, so technically, her comment had been successful.

Was the gun even loaded?

Franklin seemed kind of irresponsible. Would a good parent

keep a loaded gun in a house with somebody like him around? What if he accidentally shot out his eye?

Did Mildred have a secret pocket in her apron where she stored the gun? Did she hurriedly put on the apron when she heard the doorbell...or did she keep the apron on *at all times just in case she needed to shoot somebody?*

Oh my God, I was being held at gunpoint by a woman who carried a gun in her apron at all times just in case somebody needed to be shot.

No way was I standing up.

Adam screamed again. At least I knew he wasn't dead.

Unless he was a zombie.

No, Mr. Click was a zombie, and he couldn't scream.

Unless Adam was a different kind of zombie. One that could scream.

All of these thoughts went through my head in about 0.00039 seconds, at which point I made my final decision to respect Mildred's gun and not try to knock it out of her hand.

"So which base should we cover tonight?" asked Mildred.

Glenn shrugged. "What are you more in the mood for? The kindness and serenity of Buddhism or the human sacrifice of the Aztecs?"

"Aztecs!" said Franklin.

"Nobody asked you," Glenn told him. "Although it's been a while since we got any use out of the sacrificial chamber. The new dagger we bought has just been lying on the air hockey table."

"I'm not sure I want to cut out anybody's heart tonight," Mildred admitted.

"I'll do the heart," said Glenn.

"Actually, it's not so much the cutting out of the heart," said Mildred. "It's more about what he said about the cannibalism thing."

"You mean you think we'll look like hypocrites if we take a bite out of the heart?" Glenn asked. "That's okay. I don't mind looking like a hypocrite."

"No, it's just that I'm not sure I'll fit into the sacrificial gown. I *have* put on weight since then. I know I should exercise more, but it's hard with everything that's going on right now. I know, I know, excuses, excuses."

"If you want to treat them with kindness, that's okay with me," said Glenn. "Although we could also store them in the freezer until you're feeling more up to it."

"We still have all of that ham in the freezer. Let's just be nice."

Franklin frowned and looked as if he were going to throw a temper tantrum like a three-year-old.

Glenn looked at Kelley and me. "Good news. Looks like our religious experience for tonight is going to be to treat you with respect and dignity. Would you like some ice cream? We have chocolate mint, french vanilla, and Neapolitan."

I really wasn't sure how to react to this, so I said, "Sure. Chocolate mint."

And then my right ear exploded.

CHAPTER 19

Mildred, Glenn, and Franklin all gasped and stepped back.

Kelley screamed.

I wasn't immediately sure what had happened, except that it felt and sounded like a water balloon filled with warm water popped next to my ear.

And then pain. Lots of it.

I clutched my ear. It wasn't completely gone, but the entire earlobe was missing along with half of the cartilage above it. What remained was a wet, sticky, mangled mess.

Most of my earlobe was on my shoulder.

Back in Donna's room, Adam screamed again, though I assume it was unrelated to my ear explosion.

I tried to stifle my own scream and accidentally bit down on my tongue so hard that I screamed.

"Did you shoot?" Glenn asked Mildred, his voice frantic. "Did you shoot him?"

"I didn't shoot anybody!"

"Then what happened to his ear?"

"I don't know! It just burst!"

"*Somebody* shot him!"

"I have the only gun, and I didn't shoot it! Did you hear it go off? Did you? Do you see any smoke?"

I pulled my hand away from my ear. I was hyperventilating in a big way. More than half of my ear was gone. What if my entire head was next?

The inside part of my right ear was ringing, but I could still hear with it. So I was mutilated but not deaf.

I tried to speak but couldn't catch my breath.

Kelley had bits of ear on her shirt.

"People's ears don't do that for no reason!" said Glenn.

Franklin clutched at his heart. "It was the Aztecs!"

Then he dropped to the floor in a dead faint. I didn't blame him. I was pretty close to fainting myself, but I successfully forced myself to remain conscious and unsuccessfully tried to force myself to remain calm.

Oh God, it hurt. Though I'd never had my ear pierced, I think the pain was like having your ear pierced a million times in a row, all over, with a dull, ear-piercing device.

Blood ran down my neck.

I had to focus. Had to at least get enough control over myself to blurt out a sentence. That cabdriver could be holding the tip of a pin right between the doll's eyes.

"You have to let me make a call," I said.

Mildred shook her head.

"I won't call the cops!" I promised. "I know who did this! I have to speak with him!"

"Satan?"

"No, not Satan." I reached into my pocket and dug out the cabdriver's business card. Zeke Geiler. "Please call this number and let me talk to him."

Mildred looked like she wanted to question the reason we would call a taxi service about an exploding ear, but instead, she walked out of the living room and returned a moment later with a phone. She dialed the number on the card and then handed the phone to me.

"Try anything sneaky, and I'll shoot your other ear off," she said.

"I'm sorry, I'm sorry, I have to do this. I can't have these on me," said Kelley, her voice a full octave higher than usual, as she picked my ear bits off of her shirt and flicked them onto the floor. She'd been strong and brave through this whole ordeal, but cartilage on your clothes is a bit much for anyone.

On the other end, the phone rang once, twice, three times…

Please answer before the crazy lady decides to shoot me, I thought.

"Hello?" asked a familiar voice on the other end of the line. A voice that sounded much more evil and villainous than it had earlier this evening.

"It's me," I said.

"I was wondering when you'd call," said Zeke. "How's your ear?"

"My ear's totally fine," I said. "Why?"

My thought process while saying that: "If he thinks the voodoo doll doesn't really work, I'll have much more leverage."

My thought process immediately after saying that: "He's going to poke the doll again to make it work! Retract statement! Retract statement!"

"Okay, I lied," I told him. "I barely have any ear left. Are you happy?"

"Send me a phone picture of your missing ear. Right now. If I don't have it in sixty seconds, the doll gets hurt again."

Zeke hung up. Ack!

"This phone has a camera, right?" I asked Mildred.

"Why would my phone have a camera? I didn't buy a camera. I bought a phone."

"Every phone made since 1974 has a frickin' camera!" I said. But this one didn't even have a touch-screen display, and I didn't see a camera lens anywhere. "Listen to me! I need a camera in the next few seconds, or I am going to *splatter*!"

"We have a Polaroid in the attic," said Glenn.

"What's a Polaroid?" I asked, not that it mattered. Franklin probably had a better phone, but he was still unconscious. Unless I could somehow stop time, there was no way I could meet the driver's deadline!

Could I stop time?

No. I couldn't stop time.

What part of me was going to explode next? My eyeball? My eyebrow? My chin? My uvula? The knuckle of my left ring finger? One of my thighs? My torso? Several inches of my lower intestine? My teeth? What if my *teeth* exploded in my mouth? I couldn't even stand having the dentist drill a tiny little spot for a filling, and now there was a very real chance that my teeth could explode all over my mouth!

I frantically hit redial and called him back.

While it rang, I gave Kelley a reassuring pat on the shoulder.

It probably would have been more reassuring if the hand doing the patting wasn't covered with blood.

Adam hadn't screamed in a while.

"Where's the picture?" asked Zeke.

"I don't have a camera," I said. "But I swear to you I'm not lying. If I hold the phone up to what's left of my ear, you can probably still hear it oozing."

"I think I should pierce the doll again just to be sure."

"No! Listen to me. The doll is way more powerful than you think! It's...it's...it's like the Red Bull version of voodoo."

"Prove it with a picture."

"I said I don't have a camera! Why are you asking me to prove to you that you have the upper hand? You've won! You've got me! What do you want?"

"I want to know that you're not just yanking me around."

"Listen, Zeke—"

"Don't call me Zeke."

"That's what's on your card."

"I don't care."

"What should I call you?"

"Don't call me anything! You don't have to use people's names to talk to them! We're not trying to bond! And it's been more than sixty seconds."

"No, no, don't do it. Believe me when I say that there isn't enough Windex in the world to clean up the mess if you aren't careful with that doll! Please, just tell me what you want. We'll get it. I promise."

"I want one million dollars."

"I can't get you a million bucks. Not gonna happen."

"One million dollars, or I shove this doll into a meat grinder."

I was willing to bet he didn't even have a meat grinder handy, but I didn't try to call him out on the fib.

"I'm sixteen years old. Where am I gonna get a million dollars?"

"That's not my problem."

"Well, it *is* your problem, because you're asking for something I can't give you. This whole thing started when we didn't have enough money to pay your fare!"

"Then you'd better come up with a good offer, kid."

"You'll go to prison," I said. "I've got your business card right here. They'll know you did it."

"What, you think I'm going to get arrested for jabbing pins into a doll? Seriously? What kind of an idiot would worry about going to jail for voodoo?"

"I can get you five hundred dollars," I said.

"I want a hundred and fifty thousand."

"Can't do a hundred and fifty thousand. I can get you six hundred."

"A hundred and twenty-five thousand."

"Seven hundred."

"One hundred thousand even."

"Seven hundred and fifty."

"I'm not going lower than one hundred thousand."

"I'm not going higher than seven hundred and fifty-five."

"Then I guess that's the end of the doll."

Kelley grabbed the phone out of my hand. "Zeke? This is Tyler's girlfriend. Do you know *anything* about this kind of negotiation? You have to ask for an amount that's within the realm of possibility, or else you're just wasting everybody's time. I don't like having my time wasted. When I feel like my time is being wasted, it makes me want to get rid of those who are wasting my time, understand? No? Okay, I'm sorry." She listened silently for a moment. "Yes, we can do that. Yes, we can be there. Thank you."

To me, she said, "We're going to deliver ten thousand dollars in thirty minutes. If we call the police, you're dead. We're meeting him at the junkyard. Cool?"

"Uh..."

"*Cool?*"

"We need more time."

"Thirty minutes. That's *perfectly fine*, right?"

"Yes, that's fine."

"Good."

"Don't hang up."

Kelley handed the phone back to me. The voodoo doll issue was taken care of, except for having no possible way of getting that much cash that quickly, but we still had the problem of the Basers. Mildred and Glenn were watching me closely. I didn't think they'd just let us casually walk out of their home.

"Zeke?" I asked, forgetting the don't-call-me-Zeke rule.

"Yeah?" Apparently he had forgotten about it too.

"In the meantime, I need you to create an aura of destruction." That sounded pretty intimidating, right? I know that if I thought there was an aura of destruction in effect, even if I wasn't sure exactly what that meant, my behavior would be much more cautious.

"A what?"

"Yep, exactly. Right now. Using voodoo, the one true religion."

"What are you talking about?"

"Let's go with burning flesh. The more charred, the better."

"Huh? What?"

"I'll let you decide that one."

"You're confusing me."

"Be creative."

"What?"

"And painful."

"I truly don't know what you're talking about," said Zeke. "Is somebody else there? Is this some kind of fake-out?"

"Fifteen seconds will be fine," I said. I hung up the phone and handed it back to Mildred. "Thanks."

"Fifteen seconds for what?" she asked.

"For the aura of destruction," I said, giving her just a hint of a smile. Or at least that was my intent. Despite my attempts to maintain a cool demeanor, my voice was all shaky and squeaky, and my face was twitchy because of, y'know, the whole shredded right ear thing. So it was probably less a hint of a smile than a grotesque grimace of agony.

"What's that?"

"It's part of the same power that blew up my ear," I said. "You should never have let me call Zeke, because now everybody in this house is under its spell. If you negatively impact my aura, your flesh will burn."

"It's true," said Kelley. "Black and crispy."

"I don't believe you," said Mildred. "What does it even mean to negatively impact your aura?"

"You're starting to do it right now."

Mildred flinched.

"I don't want to turn you and your family into burnt-out shells, but I'll do it," I warned her. "I'll cook you like a hot dog."

"You're bluffing," said Glenn.

"You think so?" I pointed to the mess of my right ear. "Just know that this could be your face."

"Except burnt," said Kelley.

"Right," I said.

"What do you want from us?" Mildred asked.

"All we want is for you to let us go," I said.

"And your car," Kelley added.

I nodded. "And your car."

"Not a chance," said Glenn.

"Really?" I asked. "Are you saying you don't believe me? Do you think I came in here with a fake ear strapped to the side of my head that I could pop on cue?"

"It wasn't on cue," said Glenn. "You were obviously very surprised when it happened."

"Right. So...you know it was real then."

"I'm not doubting that your ear exploded. I'm doubting the aurora of destruction."

"Aura."

"What'd I say?"

"Aurora."

"I meant aura. The first part of the call was clearly somebody blackmailing you with a voodoo doll, but it doesn't make sense that somebody who was blackmailing you would then turn around and do you a favor. If there'd been two separate calls, I might buy it, but you're asking us to accept a pretty big flaw in logic if you want us to believe that the blackmailer has also been nice enough to set up an aura of destruction."

"He knows that if we die here, he'll never get his money," I said, thinking as quickly as you can when you suspect that part of your brain may actually be starting to leak out of your ear hole. "He didn't do it out of kindness; it was a business requirement."

"But you said it like you were asking a favor of an administrative assistant or something," said Glenn. "The two conversations didn't naturally flow into each other. Again, I'm not doubting that the damage to your ear happened exactly how you claim, but I think the rest of the conversation was completely one-sided and that we are in absolutely no danger."

"Okay," I said. "That makes sense. I've always felt that when you're at risk of *your body burning from the inside out*, you should err on the side of caution, but I'm not going to tell you how to live your life."

Kelley lunged forward a bit, fingers curled into claws. *"Bad aura!"*

Glenn let out the most girlish scream I'd heard since that time earlier in the day when I'd let out my own girlish scream.

"I still don't believe you, but you've proven your point," he said. "We're not giving you our car."

"Bad aura!"

"But we'll drive you where you need to go. It's a minivan. We've got plenty of room."

"Yeah, I saw that in the driveway," I said. "It's kind of like the one my aunt has."

"We enjoy it."

I looked at Kelley. She nodded.

"That's fine," I said. "Now let's go get my friend out of your daughter's room."

"Are you quite sure you want to do that?" Mildred asked.

"Yes."

Mildred and Glenn glanced at each other, then shrugged.

"Oooookaaaay, if that's what you want…"

CHAPTER 20

Can you believe it? We're more than two-thirds into this story. Unless you're one of those weirdos who always skips ahead to the two-thirds point of a book, I'd like to take this opportunity to thank you for sticking with me this far.

Some of you may be reading this book for school. Not as an assigned reading project like *Lord of the Flies* or *Animal Farm*, unless you have the *coolest teacher ever*, but maybe for a book report. Which means that around this point, you're probably sweating and thinking, *Aw, man, did I ever pick the wrong book! There's no literary value at all! How am I going to write a report on this thing?*

Don't worry. I've got your back. I've crammed examples of everything your teacher wants to hear about into this one chapter. Pretty sweet, huh? Stephenie Meyer wouldn't do that for you.

The four of us (Franklin was still unconscious) walked into the hallway. As I stared at Donna's bedroom door, I couldn't help but think that when I opened it, I would bear witness to a horrific sight. [*Foreshadowing.*]

The hallway was eerily silent like a graveyard at midnight. [*Simile.*] [*Also cliché.*] It was the spookiest hallway that had ever existed in any house at any point in recorded history. [*Hyperbole.*]

I [*narrator*] was a quivering bowl of jelly [*metaphor*] as we walked down the creepy crawly corridor [*alliteration*].

"This hall reminds me of *The Shining*," I said. [*Allusion.*] [*Actually, that's probably more of a reference than an allusion. An allusion would be more subtle, like if I'd said, "I feel like I'm about to walk into Room 217."*] [*It's Room 217 in the book and Room 237 in the movie. They changed it because the hotel where it was filmed had a Room 217 but not a Room 237, and they didn't want to use a real room number, I guess because they didn't want guests to worry about a scary, naked old woman rising out of the bathtub.*]

Our footsteps squeaked like a mouse. [*Personification.*] [*Poor writing.*]

I noticed that Kelley still had a piece of my ear on her shirt. It seemed to represent how I hadn't listened to her. [*Symbolism.*]

I [*hero*] [*sort of*] reached Donna's door and thought about how you shouldn't mess with forces you don't understand [*theme*] and also about how my head and foot would feel better if only I had a cool, refreshing, raspberry ice tea Snapple [*product placement*]. I scratched the lightning-shaped scar on my forehead [*shameless rip-off of more successful authors*] [*quote unquote homage*], thought about what I was going to post on MySpace [*outdated social media reference that fails to connect with readers*] and then opened the door.

It was truly a horrific sight.

This chapter is kind of short, but a couple of earlier chapters ran long, so I think it's okay to cut this one off here.

CHAPTER 21

Adam screamed again. "Tell her to quit nibbling so hard!"

My (former) best friend without clothes was truly one of the most horrific sights I'd ever been unfortunate enough to see. I wanted to throw back my head and let out a shriek of terror that would forever reverberate through these walls.

You saw that coming, didn't you?

You've been reading all this time thinking, *Adam's not in any physical danger. It's all a big fake-out, and when Tyler opens the door, he's going to write about it like it's this shocking moment, but it's only Adam naked.*

I wish that were true. Unfortunately, the first two paragraphs of this chapter were a *lie*.

Adam lay on the bed, still wearing his jeans but no shirt. His eyes were filled with terror. And Donna had what looked like a pizza cutter, and she was rolling it up and down his chest, leaving red lines.

Black candles were everywhere, creating a creepy atmosphere and a fire hazard.

There was a dead chicken on the floor.

Also a pentagram.

And a bowl filled with, if we want to pretend that the ghastly horrors of the world don't exist, red paint.

What are you even supposed to say when you stumble into that kind of environment? Standing there for a moment in stunned silence works, which is what we did, but what about after that? Are you supposed to say, "Hey, this is wrong," or is that pretty much a given?

Adam wasn't handcuffed or tied down or anything, which was kind of odd. Usually if somebody is slicing up your chest with a pizza cutter, you try to get away.

His arms were at his sides, and he was shivering. He looked sort of paralyzed.

Kelley expressed my thoughts: "What the *hell*?"

"Excuse me, hello, you ever hear of knocking?" asked Donna. She glared at Kelley and me then addressed her parents, "I thought you were going to kill them."

"Your father and I decided against human sacrifice for the night," said Mildred.

"Well, that's lame."

"Let him go," said Glenn.

"I'm not holding him down. He's free to leave whenever he wants." Donna scooted away from him.

"Uh-huh. And I'm sure you didn't inject him with the paralyzing spider venom." Mildred sighed. "What dosage did you use?"

"The small one."

"Are you sure?"

"Yes, I'm sure! I know where to fill the hypodermic needle! Stop treating me like I'm a baby!"

JEFF STRAND

"Well, put on your shoes. We're going out."

"To Chick-fil-A?"

"No."

"We never go to Chick-fil-A anymore!"

"And we're never going back if your attitude doesn't improve," said Glenn. "Your mother said to put on your shoes. We need to take these people to meet somebody very important."

"You're really letting them live?"

"Yes. I already said that. Your mother and I don't like having to repeat ourselves."

"But they've seen our faces! They know where we live! They're looking at me right now with a pizza cutter in my hand! We can't just let them walk out of here with their heads still on!"

"They're not walking anywhere. We're driving them. Don't make me tell you again to put on your shoes."

"You cut off most of his ear! You can't let somebody go after you cut off most of his ear! You guys are stupid!"

"Not that we owe you an explanation, but we didn't cut off anything. His ear exploded. *Exploded.* From the power of voodoo. We taught you about voodoo, remember?"

"Yeah, you poke a doll and somebody's leg hurts. So what?"

"'So what' is that this young man has somebody holding a voodoo doll hostage, and that's why his ear exploded. How popular do you think you would be in school if your ears exploded?"

"I don't know. It might look kind of badass."

"That's enough!" said Mildred. "Young lady, as long as you live in our house, you will respect our rules, and when we say that there will be no human sacrifices tonight, well, that's exactly

176

what we mean." She looked more closely at Adam. "He's going to survive, right?"

"Of course he's going to survive. You didn't give me enough time to cut him deep."

"Why aren't you putting on your shoes?"

"I'm going to put on my stupid shoes! Jeez! Why are you guys always so testy? How come you never yell at Franklin to put on his shoes?"

"Because Franklin puts on his shoes when we tell him that we're leaving the house!" said Mildred. "We never have to keep telling him over and over. You're way too old for us to keep having to treat you this way. Keep up the attitude problem, and I promise we will take away the pizza cutter, the spider venom, the daggers—all of them, even the one with the hidden compartment—those special pliers that Grandma made for you, your TV, everything. All of it, gone into storage until you go to college! Don't think we don't mean it. Don't think that for one single solitary second we're kidding around, because I know exactly which storage facility we'll use, and they're open twenty-four hours a day, and I have never been more serious about anything in my life!"

Mildred and Donna stared each other down angrily. Then Donna bit her lower lip and nodded. "Okay, I'll get my shoes."

Some more of my right ear exploded.

Again, not the whole thing, but at least another inch of it came off. I screamed (and though this wasn't on my mind at the moment, thinking back, I do have to say that this house really did have some impressive soundproofing. How many times had someone screamed since we'd arrived? I'm not going to go back and count, but it was a lot, and nobody had come to investigate the noise. I'm no expert on soundproofing, but this was quality work. My most sincere compliments to the designer) and dropped to my knees.

It hurt worse this time. I guess the upper half of your ear has more nerve endings than the lower half.

As far as I knew, it was only my ear. But were there other parts inside your body that could explode without you knowing it? Maybe some crucial internal organ had popped too, and I was minutes away from death without even knowing it! This night sucked! Sucked! Sucked!

"It's gonna be okay, Tyler," said Kelley, using the bottom of her shirt to wipe blood off the side of my head. "You're going to be fine. I promise. I won't let anything happen to you."

I was going to die!

It hadn't been thirty minutes! Not even close!

I was going to die!

What had I accomplished in this life? Some good grades, a girlfriend...but had I done anything to improve the economy? Had I created any lasting works of art? Would anybody remember my high video game scores after I was gone?

I was going to die!

I'd never see my mom again. My dad. My grandparents. My friends. My teachers. The lunch lady who never openly judged me for unhealthy food choices.

I was going to die!

I didn't want to die!

But I was going to die!

I didn't deserve this. I deserved bad things to happen to me, yeah, but not this. Not death! I was too young to die! I didn't want to die when people would throw themselves on my casket and say, "He was so young! So very young! What a tragedy!" I wanted to die when people would say, "Wow, we thought that shriveled old geezer would never kick the bucket!"

And then—

Hello. My name is Herbert Gellsteinner. I am a professional ghostwriter. This does not mean that I write about ghosts. It means that I write books for people who put their names on the cover but did not actually write anything. You know that reality TV star whom you secretly suspect can't even read but who suddenly announces a seven-figure deal with a major publisher? I wrote that for her.

Sometimes there's an "As Told to _____" credit where I sit in a room with a celebrity and they babble for a few hours and I turn the transcript into a book, and sometimes I do not get credit at all, and the celebrity goes around on his book tour, saying, "No, I wrote it. I wrote it all. I'm a good writer."

Sometimes there are more tragic circumstances for my involvement, such as cases where the author really was writing their book but was not lucky enough not to die during the writing process. In those sad cases, it is my job to complete the book, because otherwise you would have to read a book that just ended with "And then—" and you would never know what happens.

However, that is not the case here. If the next part was "And then Tyler's brain exploded," well, how would he have written everything you have read so far?

No, I am writing this because I believe that teenagers are the future, and I believe that at least one of you reading these words right now will become a rich and famous celebrity, and you will sell a book for a lot of money, and you will need somebody to write it for you. Please consider me for that task. I work cheap. Very cheap. And you can yell at me all you want while I am writing. I don't care. I welcome it. I really need this. I need it bad. Please become a celebrity. Please.

—Mildred's phone rang.

She glanced at the display. "It's that Zeke guy. Should I answer it?"

"Yes, please," I said.

She pressed a button on the phone and held it to her ear. "Yes? Yes. Yes, he is. Yes. Yes, you may." She held the phone out to me. "He wants to talk to you."

I took the phone from her and held it to my nondisgusting ear. *"Why did you do that, you crazy—"*

"I'm sorry, I'm sorry," said Zeke. "That was my cat's fault. Is your ear okay?"

"No, my ear's not okay! It's all over the place, you insane—"

"I wasn't reneging on our deal, I promise. It was an accident."

"Well, be more careful, you psychotic—"

"We're still meeting at the junkyard. I do apologize for that. I'll be more careful. I just wanted to call and make sure you weren't dead."

"*No, I'm not dead, no thanks to you, you rotten piece of—*"

"I'm hanging up now."

I wanted to fling the phone to the floor and stomp on it a few times while bellowing with frustration, but that would be unproductive. "No, no, wait a second. Tell her about the aura of destruction."

"Aw, man, are you back on that again?"

"They think you're faking. Explain exactly what it does." I handed the phone to Glenn.

"Hello?" he said. "Yeah. Uh-huh. Uh-huh. Uh-huh. Uh-huh. Our eyeballs? Uh-huh. No. Okay." He hung up and slipped the phone into his pocket. "He made a pretty good case for the aura of destruction. Donna. Shoes. Now."

"We really aren't going to sacrifice them?" Donna asked.

"We've already established that," said Mildred. "Your problem is that you don't listen. All of the other teenagers of the world listen to their parents, but not ours, oh no!"

Donna's face contorted into a pout that was almost exactly like the one her brother had done earlier. But then her face quickly shifted from the not-so-threatening pout to a mucho threatening mask of rage, and she dove at me. The pizza cutter got me in the shoulder.

"Get her off me!" I shouted. "I don't want to hit a girl! I don't want to hit a girl!"

Kelley dragged Donna off me and then delivered the most

brutal punch that had ever been thrown by an honors student. Donna's head flew back, and though it remained attached, she dropped to the floor and didn't get back up.

That's right. My girlfriend knocked somebody unconscious.

I don't approve of the use of violence, and you shouldn't either…but my girlfriend knocked somebody unconscious.

Yes, it meant that in the future I'd lose more arguments than I already did, but still, I couldn't help but be a proud boyfriend. The only thing Kelley did wrong was that instead of saying something clever (*"That's* how you cut a pizza!") (That doesn't even make sense, does it?), she threw her arms around me and began to cry.

I was still proud. Then, of course, I remembered my ear and my toes and the pain, and my sense of pride was replaced by pain and panic and stuff.

"I understand why you did that," said Mildred. "Harm my children again, and I'll kill you, but I'm letting that one go. Now let's get out to the minivan, so we can go to the junkyard, so you can outwit the cabdriver, so you can get the doll back."

CHAPTER 22

Franklin was still unconscious in the living room. I don't mean to be rude, but what a freaking wuss.

Mildred and Glenn decided to leave Donna and Franklin behind, a decision of which I totally approved, but Glenn and Kelley carried Adam (now with his shirt back on) out of the house and put him on the rear seat of their dark blue minivan. The back of the van was covered with bumper stickers advertising several different religions, and the dashboard was lined with bobble-heads of religious figures who can't/couldn't possibly have been happy with that kind of depiction.

Adam could move his arms a little, so the venom was wearing off, which was good, because despite his lack of helpfulness so far, we might need him later.

Kelley and I sat in the second row of seats while Glenn drove and Mildred sat in the front passenger seat. "We need a plan," I said, holding what had once been a purple towel against my head. (It was still a towel, just not purple.)

Mildred turned around and looked at us. "Excuse me, young man, but we're right here. We can hear you."

"Not a plan against you. A plan against the driver."

"Oh. That would make more sense." She turned back around.

A small suitcase rested on my lap. It did not have ten thousand dollars inside. Instead, it contained a few newspapers (approximate value: $2.75). If Zeke actually opened the suitcase, we were pretty much solidly screwed, but my hope was that there was a way to get him to do the trade without opening it. Not likely, I know. If we'd had more time, we could have come up with a plan better than "Hope Bad Guy Doesn't Open Suitcase Containing Blackmail Money," but we didn't.

"Can you sit up yet?" I asked Adam.

Adam very slowly sat up, wincing with the effort. "Do you think spider venom has any long-term effects?"

"You mean like superpowers?"

"No, that would be a nerdy thing to ask. I meant like muscle damage."

"I don't know. Probably not."

"You're just trying to make me feel better, aren't you?"

I removed the bloody towel from my ear. "Do you think I want you to feel better?"

"Okay, point taken. So I think I have a plan to get the doll back," he said. "It's kind of crazy, but it might just work. What if we…?"

"No," I said, thirty-six seconds later.

"Are you sure?"

"No. We're not using that plan."

"But if we—"

"No. Kelley is our planner."

"I would just like to point out, and I'm not trying to be disrespectful to her intelligence or anything, but it's not like things have been all sunshiny since you asked Kelley for help…and yes, I see her eyes narrowing right now, and so I'd like to blame my comment on the venom. Kelley's awesome. I'm done talking."

"He's right, though," said Kelley. "We need a better plan."

I nodded. "But not that one."

"Oh no, of course not. God, no. Not that one."

"It would've worked," said Adam.

"No, it wouldn't have," I said. "But we can do this. We're smarter than a cabdriver. Maybe he's more street-smart than we are, since he's a cabdriver, but we're more book-smart. We can come up with a plan!"

Glenn pulled the minivan in front of the junkyard. We still didn't have a plan. Or at least a good one. We had several bad plans and several plans that would be good if we had the necessary equipment like a military tank.

Mildred dialed her phone and handed it to me. Zeke answered. "I see you. Get out of the soccer mom van. Alone. Tell them to drive away. I'm holding a hunting knife with an eight-inch blade up to the doll's throat right now, so don't try anything that makes me nervous. Understand?"

"I understand," I told him, even though, quite honestly, a tiny little pin would've worked just as well as a hunting knife with an eight-inch blade.

"Good."

I sighed and did my best to summon the necessary courage. "Wish me luck," I said.

"Why the hell would I wish you luck?" asked Zeke.

"I wasn't talking to you." I hung up the phone and gave it back to Mildred. "After I get out, you're supposed to drive away. He wasn't specific, but I don't think you have to drive all the way home or anything like that. Just park a couple of blocks away."

Kelley stifled a sob and then leaned over and gave me a passionate kiss on the lips. It was as if for one moment all of our problems had disappeared and our souls were joined as one… although I also have to say that vampires are lying to you about kissing with blood on your lips being arousing. It's really kind of gross. Don't try it.

"Be careful," said Adam. "We need you to come back in one piece."

"Seriously?" I asked. "I could be headed to my death, and you think the last thing I want to hear is a joke like that?"

"What?" Adam looked genuinely confused, and then realization hit him. "Ooohhhh. No, I wasn't trying to be funny. I honestly wasn't even thinking about your missing toes and ear. That's just what you say to people. My bad."

"Look, I know I don't have much time," I said. "And I don't want to make any big speeches because I'm pretty sure I'm not going to die. But I *am* going to put myself in a situation where the guy with my life in his hands could go into a murderous rage, so if it does come to that, I'm gonna miss you guys."

Now Adam had tears in his eyes. "We're gonna miss you too."

"So, um, I don't know how I'm going to behave if he really does decide to kill me. I'd like to think that I'll be dignified about it, but I can't promise that. What I'd like to ask is that if I do anything that you know I wouldn't want to be part of my legacy...I don't mean crying, that's okay, but if I do anything that's utterly embarrassing, just completely cowardly and pathetic, could you leave that part out when you tell people about this? I mean, you don't have to say that I acted like Conan the Barbarian or anything like that. Just don't share anything where my family would be glad I'm dead."

"We've got you covered," Adam promised.

Mildred pressed a button, and the electric rear door of the minivan slowly slid open with a loud whirring noise. I gave Kelley one last kiss and then got out of the vehicle. The electric door slowly slid closed again, and the minivan drove away, leaving me alone on the sidewalk, holding the suitcase.

It would be okay.

Certainly no harm could come to a teenage boy holding a suitcase in a high-crime area after dark.

I stood there for a moment, my heart racing, my stomach in knots, and my elbow twitching. And without a family of psychos to distract me, I had the opportunity to reflect upon how much my ear hurt.

It really hurt.

I could barely think straight. It's not as if I had been making quality decisions before my ear exploded or even before my toes launched, but this was like trying to concentrate with a million stinging fire ants squirming around in my ear canal.

I kept standing there. It would definitely be anticlimactic if I bled to death before he showed up. The rest of this book would just be blank pages. I was feeling woozy, but I'd been feeling woozy most of the night, so I didn't worry about it.

I continued to wait.

You didn't see a lot of tumbleweeds in Florida, so none blew through the empty street, but it would have been appropriate.

Still waiting.

Still waiting.

Still waiting.

At least the excruciating pain was keeping me from getting bored.

Where was he? Was he waiting for me to bleed to death so he could just swoop in and grab the suitcase? What a tacky approach. I simply couldn't respect that. And if I was going to bleed to death, it was going to be within the next two or three hours, not the next two or three minutes, so Zeke had a long wait ahead.

Still waiting.

Repeat last sentence.

And then, finally, a taxi came around the corner. I assumed it was Zeke, but until he got closer…Okay, yeah, it was Zeke. He pulled up right next to me and then shut off the engine.

He very slowly got out of the car, closed the door, folded his arms in front of his chest, and nodded at the suitcase.

"You got the money?"

"Every penny."

"That better not be filled with pennies."

"It's not."

"Where'd you get it?"

"A friend."

"Which friend?"

"You wouldn't know him."

"Name him."

"Bob."

"Bob who?"

"Bob—" *Don't say Barker! Don't say Barker!* "—Anderson." Bob Anderson was in a couple of my classes, and the chances of him giving me any money were the same as the chances that he'd give me a blood transfusion that drained him completely dry, but Zeke didn't know any of my friends.

"What does Bob Anderson do for a living?"

"He's sixteen. He works at Burger King."

"Then where did he get ten thousand dollars?"

"His parents."

"Why would his parents give him that much money to give to you?"

"I don't know. I didn't ask him for his cover story."

"If his family is so rich, why is he working at Burger King?"

"To build character."

"What's his name again?"

"Bob Anderson."

"You said Bob Henderson before."

"No, I didn't."

"Hmmmm."

"Are you trying to poke holes in my story? That's fine. I understand that, but let's get this done so we can all go home. I'm sure you have better things to do, and I'd kind of like to get to a hospital, so let's quit wasting time and make this deal happen!" I was trying to sound like a tough guy. You'd have to get somebody else's opinion on my level of success.

Zeke tilted his head. "Wow. I really *did* mess up your ear."

"Yep."

"Or did you do it yourself? You scamming me? You cutting up your ear to make me think it's voodoo?"

"Is this really the way you behave?" I asked. "I mean, is this the way you spend your nights, trying to drive people to the brink of madness? Am I on one of those hidden-camera shows? Are you trying to get millions of hits on YouTube? Seriously, dude, what's your deal?"

He frowned. "I'm new to this."

"Well, you suck at it."

"Got any Red Bull?"

"No."

"Okay. Set the suitcase down at your feet and then open it."

I didn't much want to do that.

Zeke smiled. "If you've got anything you want to confess before you open it, now's the time to speak up."

"The money's there," I said.

"Good. Then we'll have no problems. If I see anything in there but cash, it's all over for you. Set it down. Now!"

And then...I came up with a plan.

It was not a brilliant plan. You're not going to think that I'm some sort of plan-making genius. But I realized that maybe, just maybe, I might make it out of this.

I quickly reviewed my plan for opportunities for disaster. There were lots of them. Still, I had to do something, and this was the best I could come up with. If I died, well, at least I died while making an effort not to die.

Zeke's tone quickly changed from annoyingly suspicious to angry. "I said, put it down!"

I wiped a big smear of blood from my head onto my palm and showed it to him. "I'm bleeding out of my head because of you. You're lucky I can even stand. Give me a break, okay?"

I leaned down, making a medium-sized show of the effort it took to crouch down. I set the suitcase on the cement and then began to wobble.

"Dizzy spell," I said. "Hold on a second."

"You don't have a second. Open the suitcase."

I coughed a few times, then wiped my forehead as if I were sweating and then said, "Oh God," and collapsed.

"You faking it?" Zeke asked.

I didn't answer.

"I know you're faking. I'm not that stupid. If you're faking, I'll kill you."

Because it had already been established that he was going to kill me if the suitcase didn't have his cash, this threat did not encourage me to reveal my ruse.

"I can wake you up, no problem," said Zeke. "You want me to twist this doll's arm around a few times? That what you want?

How about just the wrist? How about a twist of the wrist and then I keep twisting until its entire arm looks like a Red Vine? You cool with that?"

I wasn't cool with that at all, but I didn't say anything. This was my only chance. (I told you it wasn't a brilliant plan.)

Here's the psychology I was hoping for: Zeke was not a bad guy at heart. He was no sweetheart. He wouldn't be winning any Best Person Ever awards, but deep inside, he tried to be a decent human being. But he was struggling financially, and the opportunity presented to him by the voodoo doll along with his natural fury over the fact that we couldn't pay our fare was too much for him to resist.

Yes, he was the kind of jerk who would make my ear explode. But that was from a distance. When he did that, he couldn't see the results of his nonhumanitarian behavior. Could he really turn my arm into a mangled mess with me right there in front of him?

It suddenly occurred to me that I didn't know the guy at all. Maybe he *could* turn my arm into a mangled mess with me right there in front of him. Maybe with a great big smile on his face. Maybe he'd buy some balloons afterward.

I remained motionless.

I heard the door to the cab open and then close again.

"I've got the doll in my hand," Zeke informed me. Was that hesitation in his voice? Was he discovering the kindness in his heart?

"I'm going to twist it," he reminded me.

I remained motionless.

"You're not going to like it when I twist it."

I suddenly felt as if I needed to hiccup. That was kind of weird, because I'd never felt as if I *needed* to hiccup before. I always just hiccupped. The body does odd things in moments of severe stress.

I resisted the urge to hiccup.

The other thing I hoped was that Zeke would decide that the injured teenager lying on the sidewalk did not pose a threat. I sure didn't feel like a threat. If I were Zeke, and I saw me lying there looking the way I looked, I would've just strolled on over and grabbed the suitcase.

"I mean it," said Zeke.

Oh yeah, he was totally hesitating. I had him exactly where I wanted him. I was the *king* of faking unconsciousness because of blood loss.

As I heard his footsteps, I silently summoned every ounce of strength I had. It wasn't many ounces.

"You're about to feel a lot of pain," he told me.

And then I did.

But—joy, joy, joy—it wasn't because any body parts were going kablooey or detaching themselves. He was stepping on my hand. Hard. It hurt bad enough to make me wince and give away that I was faking, but not bad enough to keep me from grabbing the suitcase and bashing it into his knee.

He let out such a loud bellow that you would've thought half of the poor guy's ear had exploded. I swung the suitcase back the other way, connecting with the same knee.

The doll dropped onto the sidewalk.

Zeke lunged his foot toward it, trying to squish it flat, but I bashed him with the suitcase again. The suitcase popped open, spilling crumpled up newspapers everywhere.

I hit him again, and Zeke fell.

I quickly got to my feet, raised the suitcase above my head with both hands, and then...well, you can't beat somebody to death with a suitcase, even if it's a scumbag blackmailer like Zeke. It's just not right.

"Get out of here," I told him.

Zeke got up and ran, limping badly. I wanted to throw the suitcase at him, knocking him down in a hilarious slapstick manner, but then he might pick up the suitcase, say, "Ha ha, now *I've* got the weapon!" and come back and beat me to death with it.

So I let him go.

He ran, slipped, fell, got back up, then ran some more. I picked up the voodoo doll, brushed some dirt off it, and let out a happy little cheer.

I had it back!

If I'd had full use of my feet, I swear I would've danced a jig right there. Instead, I settled for a quick, funky shuffle.

I looked over at the minivan and (very gently) waved the doll in the air. The minivan's engine started back up. It pulled away from the curb and drove...away from me.

Hmmm. That was odd.

I wondered why they hadn't come back to pick me up, and then I remembered, oh yeah, Kelley and Adam were trapped in a minivan with a pair of psycho killers.

CHAPTER 23

There are many difficult decisions in life.

For example, let's say that you're working in a coal mine, and it collapses. You and five other miners are trapped in a small pocket, and you have about one hour of air before you all suffocate. Rescuers will never reach you in an hour.

One other miner, Jimbo, was separated from everybody else in the collapse. He has plenty of air, enough air to last for weeks, even if he pants a lot.

There's a small gap in your pile of rocks.

You have a hand grenade.

Do you throw the hand grenade through the gap, blowing up Jimbo but ensuring your own rescue? Six lives versus one. But can you kill an innocent man to save your own lives, especially knowing that Jimbo would almost certainly be rescued?

Actually, I guess that any gap big enough for a grenade would be big enough to let in air. And a grenade wouldn't actually clear out fallen rocks; that's really a job better suited for dynamite. I don't think this is the way the hypothetical dilemma is supposed to go. I remember that when a friend posed it to me once, I was like, "Wow, that's a really difficult decision!" but the way I've got it doesn't make much sense.

Okay…so…eating one of your fellow miners. A difficult decision, right? You don't want to do it too early, because if you get saved, you all look like a bunch of jerks, but if you wait too long, you could all die with perfectly good arm meat available.

I see that I have completely botched the point I was trying to make, but basically, what I'm trying to say is that life is filled with difficult decisions.

The decision to go after the minivan was not one of them.

Kelley and Adam needed my help. Yeah, I needed help too, but I was going to rescue them, no matter what.

I got in the taxi. He'd never shut off the meter, and we owed him over three hundred dollars at this point. Maybe when all of this was over, I'd write him a check…in *blood*! (Sorry, but that's as badass as I get.)

I'd never driven a taxi before, but I assumed it was just like a regular car. I fastened my seat belt, floored the accelerator, and sped down the street in the direction the minivan had gone.

They weren't gonna get away.

Not a chance.

When I looked back on this evening, I knew I was going to have a lot of regrets (see everything else that happened in this book), but one of them was *not* going to be that I'd let Whack-Job Mildred and Totally Bonkers Glenn get away with Kelley and Adam.

The camera flashed as I sped through a red light.

Ha! Ticket for Zeke!

The minivan was a few blocks ahead. Now that I'd found it, I had to solve the more difficult problem of how to stop it.

Did I need to stop it? What if I just followed it until it stopped on its own? They were probably headed back home to pick up Donna and Franklin.

But if they knew I was following, Mildred might crawl into the backseat of the minivan and kill Kelley and Adam.

If I tried to follow without being seen, I might lose them.

If Mildred killed them, it might not be a simple stab-stab-and-it's-over death. Human sacrifices could linger.

I had to stop that minivan, no matter what.

The minivan had a lead, but it was built for fuel efficiency and passenger space, while the cab was built for *speed*. I rocketed down the street, not even thinking about my hideous injuries and the fact that I would probably spend the rest of my life with a nickname like One-Eared, Eight-Toed Tyler. The pain didn't matter. Getting blood on Zeke's seat was amusing but didn't matter. Oxygen and sunlight didn't matter. Nothing mattered except stopping that minivan! I wish we had the budget to put that sentence in 3-D, because I really can't emphasize enough how nothing else mattered.

I narrowed the distance between us from four blocks to three blocks to two blocks to one block to half a block to a quarter of a block to an eighth of a block back to a quarter of a block because I didn't want to ram them, and then I pulled into the opposite lane and sped up alongside the vehicle, doing fifty-five.

Glenn looked over at me and then rolled down his window. I couldn't lean over and roll down the passenger side window while

I was speeding down the street in the wrong lane, so hopefully he'd shout whatever he had to say loud enough for me to hear.

Mildred handed him something.

I applied the brakes as I saw the gun.

He put his hand out the window and shot at me. A hole appeared in the center of the windshield, and the bullet punched into the seat right next to me.

Despite this noteworthy increase in the amount of my personal danger, I did not veer from the nothing-else-matters attitude. I did, however, veer out of that particular lane and swerve into the correct lane, right behind the minivan.

I could see Adam peering out the rear window, looking most frightened indeed. I was dangerously close. If they decided to slam on the brakes, I'd be screwed. I eased off the gas a bit.

A huge semi whizzed past us in the opposite lane. It was a good thing that I'd already switched lanes, or that would have posed a pretty big problem.

I knew that if I rammed it from behind, the damage to the taxi would be a lot worse than the damage to the minivan. (Actually, I knew no such thing from any kind of experience, but it sounded reasonable.) They'd drive off, and I'd be left with a wrecked cab.

So my only choice was to pull up alongside again and ram them right off the road. Yes, Glenn had a gun, but I knew that if I were driving a minivan at high speed with two hostages in the back, my aim would suck. If I did this quickly, he wouldn't have a chance to get off a good shot.

I could do this.

I wasn't scared at all, I told myself.

Myself didn't believe me.

A tiny voice of self-preservation said, *Gosh, I think Kelley and Adam will be just fine if you take no action to rescue them,* but I told the voice to shut the hell up. Not out loud.

I floored the accelerator.

Up ahead, maybe two blocks, I could see that the road ended. You either turned left, turned right, or smashed into a very large brick building.

I had to get this done.

I sped up alongside the vehicle ahead, and this time, Glenn's bullet went through the passenger window. I couldn't tell where it hit, but it hadn't struck me or the doll, so I didn't care.

I yanked the steering wheel to the right. For a split second, I started to think that maybe the little voice that had advised a different course of action had a point, but only for a split second.

The two vehicles collided.

The minivan went off the road and onto the sidewalk. In case you had any moral issues with this, I should remind you that the streets were eerily devoid of people. I wouldn't have done it if there were any pedestrians. I hope you already knew that.

The taxi went out of control and swerved back into the wrong lane. I slammed on the brakes and heard a loud crash and a honk. As the taxi screeched to a stop, I looked over and saw that the minivan had smashed into the side of a brick building right after taking out a fire hydrant. A huge spray of water jettisoned into the air. I could now cross *Smash a minivan into a fire hydrant like in an over-the-top action movie* off my bucket list.

Now what? The minivan was stopped.

It would be kind of silly to go through all the trouble of crashing it only to run over there and get shot. I mean, there's a line between heroic and suicidally reckless. I didn't want my tombstone to say *Here Lies Tyler Churchill. He Should Have Stopped after the Minivan Crashed and Not Run toward It When the Driver Still Had a Gun.*

The rear door slowly slid open.

Mildred fell out.

Kelley climbed out and gave me a thumbs-up sign. I assumed this meant that Adam was also not dead and that Glenn was not actively shooting at anybody.

I'd done it! I'd saved them!

And then, suddenly, a new voice: *What in the freaking frack were you thinking by running them off the road! You could have killed them! What kind of recklessly irresponsible person are you? Don't ever do that again!*

I vowed that I would not do this ever again. The next time my friend and girlfriend were kidnapped, I would allow the proper authorities to handle the situation, using their training and years of experience.

Apparently what happened is Glenn was not wearing his seat belt. I know what you're thinking: *What? Seriously? With kidnap victims loose in the back of the vehicle and the high probability of a high-speed chase, the fool wasn't wearing his seat belt? How does that even happen?* Well, to be fair, he *was* wearing the seat belt during the drive from their home to the junkyard, but while they were parked waiting for me to resolve my issues with the taxi driver, he took off his seat belt for comfort.

Then when Zeke ran off, Glenn said, "Ha ha! We're not going to pick up your friend! Instead we're driving away so my wife and I can torture you to death!" (I don't know if that exact phrasing was used, and the "Ha ha!" part seems unlikely, but that was the gist.) Glenn was so excited about this wicked twist of events that he forgot to buckle up for safety.

So, when the minivan struck the building, Glenn struck the steering wheel, giving it a good solid honk right before his sternum broke. When somebody is trying to kill you, believe me, it's always better for you if his or her sternum breaks.

Mildred was wearing her seat belt. This made it more difficult for Kelley to drag her out of her seat and knock her unconscious as she had her daughter, but Kelley got the seat belt unfastened and managed just fine.

Adam got out of the vehicle as well.

Kelley and Adam were safe. I had the doll back. And the cab wasn't broken, so we had a means of transportation to get to Esmeralda's House of Jewelry.

I gave Kelley a hug and then said, "Wait a second. We should grab Mildred's phone before—"

A gunshot rang out.

"Fudge!" I shouted. (Not really, but you can use context clues to figure it out.) Without saying anything else, the three of us knew that it was best to ditch the retrieve-the-phone plan and resort to the get-into-the-cab-before-the-psycho-with-the-broken-sternum-shoots-us plan.

Another gunshot, and then Kelley cried out and fell to the ground.

CHAPTER 24

Four days later…

"It is a great tragedy," said the reverend, gesturing to the casket. "Such a great, great tragedy, one that causes intense sadness in all who hear of it. It was too soon for the person in that casket to be taken from us, far too soon, and the lives of all who knew that person are now poorer as a result of that person's untimely death."

Everybody at the funeral sniffled sadly.

"Some of you may be angered by the passing of this person. You think it's a dirty trick. You think, 'Noooo, they weren't supposed to die! There were much better choices for who should have died instead!'" The reverend lowered his head. "I agree with you. This is not a satisfying death by any stretch of the imagination, and if an author ever turned this life into a book and killed this person off at this point, I would throw the book against the wall and never read anything else by that author for the rest of my life. Why do authors feel the need to kill off characters we like? It's as if they're thinking, 'Oooh! Oooh! Look at me! I'm so dangerous that I can kill off a character and basically spit in your face for having an emotional investment in them!'"

"Hear, hear!" said a sad person in the front row.

Somebody threw themselves onto the casket and sobbed and screamed, "It's just not fair!" while pounding on the lid.

Everybody kept crying for a long time.

Three months ago…

I stared at Kelley, whose name I thought was Kaylie, from across the hallway. I knew I could spend the rest of my life with her, if she'd let me. She was beautiful, smart…and unattainable. I could never have somebody like her. I was best suited for the kinds of girls who only liked you because you could borrow your mom's car sometimes.

"Go say something," Adam urged.

"She'd never talk to me."

"Of course she will. She may not say anything positive, but she won't pretend you don't exist. Go on. What's the worst that can happen?"

"She could knife me."

"She's not going to knife you. Worst-case scenario, she tasers you. Isn't the risk of being tasered worth the chance to talk to her, even if it makes you pee in front of everybody?"

"No. Nothing is worth public peeing."

"Fair enough, but let's be real. She's not going to whip out a taser. The real worst-case scenario is that it's a little awkward and then you move on with your life. Do you know anybody whose social life was destroyed because they talked to a girl who wasn't interested?"

"Yes. Hector."

"Hector doesn't count. He asked a cheerleader to floss him. You're not going to say anything disturbing, so you'll be fine. I promise."

I took a deep breath. Adam was right. The benefits far outweighed the risks.

I walked across the hallway. She closed her locker, saw me, and smiled.

"Hi," I said. "I'm Tyler."

One hundred and thirty-seven years later, in a future where humankind has finally learned the dangers of making technology too cool...

"All hail the robots!" shouted Human #9,213,671.

"Hail!" shouted the crowd.

"Who controls our every move with kindness and respect?"

"The robots!"

"Who disintegrates only those who deserve it?"

"The robots!"

"Who will we overthrow?"

"The robots!" shouted Human #3,008,502. He slammed his hand over his mouth as he realized that it was a trick question. An instant later, a giant green laser disintegrated him.

"All hail the robots!"
"All hail the robots!"

One hundred and thirty-six years and nine months earlier...

A gunshot rang out.

Kelley cried out and fell to the ground, clutching her thigh.

My fear was replaced by anger. *Nobody* shoots my girlfriend! Especially not after I just saved her.

"Go! Go! Get in the cab!" Adam told me, reaching down to take Kelley by the arm. "I've got this!"

I appreciated his selfless gesture, but no. I'm not trying to imply that I wouldn't care if I got shot, but I was going to do everything I could to make sure Kelley didn't get shot a second time.

As we pulled her to her feet, I saw a long red streak across her outer thigh. It didn't look that bad. I mean, by the standards of a teenage girl's average daily life, which didn't usually include gunshot wounds, it was a big deal, but by the standards of this evening, I'd seen much worse than a bullet ripping across somebody's leg.

After today, everything would be easy. Pop quiz? Hey, not as bad as having five thugs point guns at you! Grounded for a week? Could be worse, like losing body parts! Can't get a date for the prom? Quit whining and happily think about the fact that you aren't currently having a pizza cutter applied to your chest! My life was nothing but ease and relaxation from now on.

Glenn fired again. I'm not sure what he hit, if anything, but it wasn't any of our bodies.

Kelley was hurt, but she could hop just fine, and we got her into the back of the cab. I scooted in after her, and Adam scooted in after me, shutting the door behind him.

"Somebody needs to drive," I told him.

"Oh yeah."

Adam crawled over us, only jostling two of our injured areas in the process, and then got out on the side of the cab that was safer from bullets. He got in the driver's side and adjusted the rearview mirror, and then we sped off.

We'd done it! We weren't in top-notch physical condition, but three out of three of us were still alive! That was a passing score!

"It's not that bad," I told Kelley, inspecting her wound. "It's just like a cat scratch, except maybe one where the cat's claws are the size of, I don't know, a dinosaur tooth. You'll need stitches, but we'll get matching stitches. That'll be neat. Are you going into shock?"

"Not yet."

"Do you need to go to the hospital before we take care of the doll?"

Kelley violently shook her head. "Absolutely not. After all we've been through, there's no way we're not going to solve the problem we came out here to fix. I'll be fine."

"I feel kind of bad that I'm the only one not seriously hurt," said Adam. "Only the pizza cutter, which wasn't as bad as you'd think. It's almost like I should stab myself in the knee or something."

"Be my guest," I said.

"After the car is stopped," Kelley clarified.

"Do you think the cops are looking for us?" Adam asked.

"I assume so."

"Do you think they're going to be mad?"

"Probably. Still, I think we're okay. There's a lot of stuff that's going to be really difficult to explain, but it still comes down to belief in the supernatural, which I don't think we're going to get from the police. And if they don't believe the voodoo element, then we haven't committed any crimes."

"We just stole a taxi," Adam said.

"Shut up," I said, "Even with all of the bizarre stuff that's happened, if we get rid of the doll, there's no proof of anything supernatural, right?"

"Except Zombie Click in the sewer," said Kelley.

"Dammit!"

"Can that be traced back to us?" Adam asked.

"Yeah, I mean, I'm sure it can," I said, "but it's not against the law to dump a zombie into the sewer. He was trying to strangle you. When a dead guy tries to strangle you, you throw him down a manhole, right?"

"Right, but we weren't talking about whether it's legal to do that; we were talking about evidence of the supernatural. I mean, I guess they could rule that he was alive all along and it was a clerical error…"

"You know what, maybe he'll never be found," I said. "If I'm a cop and a dead teacher disappears from the morgue, I'm not going to say, 'Let's search the sewer!' How hard will they even look? If a dead body disappears, do you put out an

APB, or do you just sort of, I don't know, check the closets and move on?"

"I think they'd look pretty hard for a missing cadaver."

"Why?"

"Would you want to admit to a dead person's family that you lost the body? As a patient, would you feel comfortable going to a hospital with a history of losing bodies? If they can't keep track of a dead body, how can they keep track of the sick ones that are still alive?"

"I guess you're right," I admitted.

"And why are we assuming that he was dead—I mean dead-dead, not living dead—when he left? For all we know, he sprang to life and went on a rampage. He could have left a trail of destruction. The hospital corridors could be littered with corpses."

"Great."

"I'm just keeping it real."

"How else are you planning to make me feel better? Should we talk about gangrene again? Oh gosh, I'm a little woozy. I sure hope it's not a tumor. How many nuclear missiles do you think are pointed at us right now? Do you think the sun is ever going to just stop working?"

"Are you two done?" Kelley asked.

Adam nodded. "I was *born* done."

"What?"

"Oh. Sorry. I don't even know what that meant."

"If you guys can stop…I don't even know what it is you're doing. It's not real talking. I wanted to let you know that we're almost there."

"I knew that," said Adam.

"You should. You've been here twice."

"I know. I'm just reminding you that I'm on top of things."

"Well, thank you."

"No problem."

We were finally on Duncan Street, which was lined with plenty of lame little shops that I would never personally visit, because I don't like stores that suck.

We drove past snooty shop after snooty shop. There were a few people wandering around but not nearly as many as I would have expected. A shopping district like this shouldn't have had this many available parking spaces. Weird.

And there it was: Esmeralda's House of Jewelry. A tiny little store with a barely legible sign sandwiched between a coffee shop and another coffee shop. Our quest was over.

Adam pulled the taxi into a parking space right in front of the store and shut off the engine. "You guys mind if I wait in the car?"

CHAPTER 25

"Are you kidding?" I asked.

Adam shrugged. "I just don't see why it takes three of us to do this. The doll isn't very heavy."

"What are you afraid of, Adam?"

"Nothing."

"There's something."

"Nothing. I'm only being practical. The cab is stolen. What if the driver comes back for it? Who will defend it?"

"If he manages to find us, I think we can let it go."

"I'm not trying to get out of going in there or anything," Adam said. "All I'm saying is that we don't need all three of us. That's all. No big deal. And I figured that you probably wanted to go to make sure it was done right, and Kelley would want to go with you because she's your girlfriend, and so maybe we didn't need to all go, know what I mean? You guys can do this just as well as I can."

"I have a bullet hole in my leg, Adam," said Kelley.

"It's not a hole. It's a scrape."

"Call it a scrape again. I quadruple dare you."

"Okay, it's a groove. You've got a big groove in your leg. If you didn't want to walk into the store, I'd totally understand. I wouldn't want to walk in there either in your condition. I was paying you a compliment by saying that you *would* want to walk in there even though you got shot in the leg. When you said you didn't need to go to the hospital, I was impressed! I thought, wow! I wouldn't want to stand in the way of that kind of devotion."

I stared at him. "I think that is the most babbling I've ever heard a person do. It's like every sentence you say gets more and more desperate. What's wrong with you?"

"Please don't make me go in there."

"You're coming with us." I opened the car door. "If you try to run, I swear, hurt foot or not, I will take you down."

Adam sadly opened the driver's side door and got out of the cab. Kelley and I got out as well. I held the voodoo doll very carefully, because losing it with six or seven steps to go to our destination would be beyond lame.

I had no idea what was going on with Adam, but I couldn't help but suspect that there was some sort of unpleasant revelation awaiting us when we entered the store.

We pushed open the door. A small bell above the door tinkled. The shop was very tiny, consisting of little but two long display cases of jewelry. Behind the counter was a beaded curtain. The place smelled like incense mixed with mildew mixed with Lysol mixed with a cheeseburger that should have been eaten much sooner than now.

"We're closed," said a voice that sounded like it belonged to the oldest, croakiest, phlegmiest woman in the world. It came from behind the curtain.

"My name is Kelley," said Kelley. "I called earlier."

The woman pushed through the beaded curtain. She was dressed entirely in black, except for her immense amount of gaudy jewelry. She looked about eighty years younger than she sounded, meaning she looked about forty.

"You called about the doll?" she asked.

"Yes."

"Well, where have you been for crying out loud? Do you think I have nothing better to do than stand around all night waiting for you? You said you'd be right over! This wasn't right over!"

"We're sorry."

"You're lucky Gordon Ramsay isn't on tonight, or you'd be out of luck. So you've got a doll problem, huh?"

"Yes. Like I said on the phone, you sold our friend a voodoo doll, and we need its power taken away."

"Voodoo?"

"Voodoo."

The woman snorted. "Calling my practice voodoo is an insult to true Haitian *Vodou*. This has nothing to do with the supreme god *Bondye*, nor are there any *loa* involved, and I'm as much of a *mambo* as you are a member of the Blue Man Group. Even if we extended the definition to include New Orleans voodoo, where's the *Legba*? Where's the *gris-gris*? Why don't you do a little research?"

Kelley remained calm, though it was clearly not easy. "Do you sell dolls that are *like* what somebody would call a voodoo doll?"

"On occasion. Maybe. Touristy stuff. Who wants to know?"

"I do."

"I don't know who you are. My eyesight is terrible. I literally can't see more than six inches in front of my face. Come up real close and state your business."

The three of us looked at each other. Well, Kelley and I did. Adam was looking at the floor.

Do you think she can hurt us? I mouthed to Kelley.

She seems harmless, Kelley mouthed back.

What if there's a trapdoor? I mouthed.

Kelley shrugged. *I think we have to trust her.*

I mouthed back something that would have been blurred on television.

What else were we supposed to do? We couldn't just walk out of the place and hope that we happened to stumble upon some other lady who could deactivate a voodoo doll. We had to trust that this woman was not going to whack off our heads with a machete.

Despite all of the homicidal people we'd encountered, I wasn't getting a *I'm gonna kill you* vibe from this woman. It wouldn't surprise me at all if she said, "Come closer...closer...closer... clooooooosssssssseeeeerrrrrr," and then when we were only a couple of inches away went "BOO!!!" but I didn't think she'd try to slay us.

We walked up to the counter.

The woman's eyes widened, and she pointed at the side of my head. "Holy cow, kid, your ear is *pulped*! Why aren't you at a hospital?"

"We need your help first," I said.

"Are you crazy? You can't be walking around with your ear like that! You need medical attention! At least put some ice on it for Pete's sake!"

"It's fine," I assured her.

"Are you not seeing the same thing I'm seeing?" The woman turned to leave. "I'm calling an ambulance!"

"No! Please! We really need your help."

"Doesn't that hurt?"

"Yes. Bad." I set the doll on the counter. "Please, whatever you did to this, I need you to undo."

The woman turned back around and inspected the doll. "I didn't do anything to that."

I bit down on the sides of my mouth to keep from screaming in frustration. Was it really so much to ask to have one, just one conversation tonight that didn't make me want to rip out every single piece of hair on my head and then paint over my scalp so that new hair couldn't grow back in its place?

(Yes, that's the exact thought I had at the time.)

The beaded curtain rustled, and another woman pushed her way through. She was dressed in similar black clothing and wore similar gaudy jewelry but looked like she could be the other woman's great-great-great-great-great-grandmother.

"Who do you speak to?" she asked, her voice raspy but otherwise pleasant. Her face lit up as she looked past us. "It is he!"

"Who?" I asked. I glanced back at Adam. "Him?"

She ignored my question and picked up the voodoo doll. "Ah, yes. The doll I make." She tapped the side of its head. "It hurt your ear, yes?"

"Yes!"

"Good, good."

"No, not good. It also killed two of my toes."

"Yes. Very powerful magic. Very powerful."

"We want the magic gone," I said. "It's too powerful. I don't like having a doll that can do this to me. You made it too strong."

The woman smiled. "My magic very small," she said, holding her index finger and thumb a tiny bit apart. Then she pointed at Adam. "*His* magic huge." She threw her hands apart, miming an explosion. "Kaboom!"

"What?" I asked.

Adam continued to stare at the floor.

"He add to power of doll. Make it super-magical. He Chosen One."

"*What?*"

"He Adam Westell, who will stop conquest of the hobgoblins."

"Ma'am, I don't mean to be disrespectful," I said, "but he's not the Chosen One. He's a dork."

The woman glared at me. "You regret harsh words when hobgoblins gnaw on your bones! They suck out marrow! They dine upon kidneys! He will save world! He come in asking for doll of teacher. I, Esmeralda, give him doll of teacher. His magic make my magic stronger. I see what it do on television. Teacher leg come off. He come back in and ask for doll of you. I not want to make doll, but not want to piss off Chosen One. Want to be on savior of humanity's good side. Make doll. It work good, yes?"

"What makes you think he's the savior of humanity?" asked Kelley. The idea did not seem to enthuse her.

"Look like him."

"Okay."

"I give him doll for eighty dollars. Not tell him he Chosen One, and he not ask why he get such good deal. Take Chosen One blood to make very powerful syrup. He come back, wanting new doll. I tell him destiny. Give him complimentary doll. You so smart, you doubt status as Chosen One, then explain to me extreme doll power?"

Esmeralda had a point about the doll, but the concept of Adam saving the world was going to take me a few decades to process.

"I cast spell of protection. Slight dimensional shift. Things not normal. Safer."

"Safer?" I asked. "We were anything *but* safe tonight!"

"You go into bad neighborhood. Without spell of protection, you dead in thirty seconds. Spell not work perfect, maybe cause some strange things to happen, but overall, safer."

"This is insane."

"Keep blood from coming out as fast. You still alive, yes?"

"Can you remove its power?" I asked. "The Chosen One doesn't want any more of my body parts to fly off."

"You sarcastic," said Esmeralda. "I should kick doll across room."

"No, no, no, I apologize. I've known Adam for a long time, and I never really thought of him in that way, but every flower needs to bloom, I guess. I feel protected from the hobgoblins already."

"We promise to worship Adam as much as you want," said Kelley. "But please, can you take away the doll's power?"

"Chosen One must ask."

Adam walked over to the counter. "It would be really cool if you'd turn it back into a regular doll."

"So I shall. Simple spell. Take fifteen, twenty seconds at most."

I breathed a sigh of relief.

"Spell do require sixteen inches of intestine from afflicted party."

"I beg your pardon?"

"Lower intestine, though. Not big deal. Large intestine removal hurt, but you no miss lower intestine much."

"I hope you're kidding," I said.

Esmeralda nodded. "Yes. Gypsy magic not humorless. Recite words, wave hands, spell over. My daughter's role entirely with mind. Easy spell."

"Thank God."

"All I need is original doll and original victim."

"Excuse me?"

"First doll." She held up my doll. "This second doll. Need both to remove spell."

"We didn't bring the other doll," I said. "It's at my house."

"Pity."

I closed my eyes and took several deep, calming, soothing breaths. When I opened my eyes again, my life still sucked. "Okay. We'll get the other doll. I guess it was silly for us to think that we wouldn't have further need of the doll after Mr. Click's neck got broken."

"Sarcasm again. I impale doll on car antenna."

"I apologize again." I rubbed my forehead to ease the oncoming headache and tried to convince myself that this was no big deal. "This is no big deal," I said. "No big deal at all. I know exactly where the doll is, and we'll just go get it, bring it back, and...did you say first victim?"

"Yes."

"You mean my history teacher?"

"Yes."

"You need us to bring you Mr. Click?"

"Yes. Tall order, admittedly."

"Why didn't your daughter tell me any of this on the phone?" Kelley asked.

"She not phone person. Too impersonal. She not fan of texting either. I think is good. Have skilled thumbs."

"Great."

"You not first teenagers to steal dead body. Pose as medical students. Girl distract security guard with beauty. Put history teacher on gurney and cover with sheet. Look like you know what you doing when you wheel gurney to exit. Nobody stop you."

"He's not in the morgue anymore," I said. "He came after us! Came after Adam, actually."

Esmeralda frowned. "That interesting."

"His leg was back on, and he was running around, and he kept trying to strangle Adam!"

"He probably have unfinished business. Like I say, my spell make strange things happen. This odd side effect. Not easy for cadaver to escape morgue and hospital and run down streets of city, chasing after victim without attracting attention. Kudos to Chosen One's natural ability to enhance spell."

"He's in the sewer," I said.

"Why he look for Adam in sewer?"

"No, we put him there."

"Disrespectful to educator."

"He was trying to strangle the Chosen One," I said. "What else were we supposed to do?"

"Maybe he not trying to strangle. Maybe he trying to hug Chosen One's neck."

"Are you kidding again?" I asked.

"Yes. I make jolly."

"So what you're saying is that we have to drag Mr. Click out of the sewer and bring him back here."

"That basic gist, yes. But that easier than original morgue plan, so when you think about it, living dead teacher good thing. Go. We care for doll while you gone. Not let monkeys steal it. We do spell when you return."

The other woman, who'd said nothing since Esmeralda came out and, now that I think of it, had kind of looked like she was in a trance the entire time, blinked. "When they return?"

"Yes. When they...oh no..."

"I thought we were starting now."

"No."

"I'm sorry. I thought these kids would appreciate that I went ahead and got started. And when I go into the dazed state, I don't really hear anything."

Esmeralda returned her attention to me. "Small problem that I think you no like," she said. "Spell already in progress. My sister not aware of complications involving other doll and first victim that we discuss earlier. You now have, how you say, ticking clock."

"What kind of ticking clock?"

The younger woman took over. "Think of it as being like the

alarm clock you use to wake yourself up in the morning to go to school. Except that instead of making a beeping sound, it causes your body to incinerate from the inside out and banishes your soul to hell."

"I...would not enjoy that alarm," I said.

"Maybe it's not specifically hell. Someplace very similar, though. Lakes of fire for sure."

"I don't want to be rude," I said, wanting very much to be rude, "but if the risk of hellfire was involved, do you think maybe you could have *verified* that it was time to start the spell beforehand?"

"Most people who seek enchanted objects actually want them to do what they're supposed to. We don't get a high return rate. I empathize with your plight, but it's not my fault that you dabbled in the dark arts without being ready to commit."

I said, "I didn't—" and then decided that I should stop talking. My sense of moral outrage at their poor customer service had to take a backseat to the race against time to avoid internal incineration.

"How long do we have?" Kelley asked.

"From when I started the spell? About an hour and a half. So let's say ninety minutes minus a couple of minutes. I've never been one to interfere in other people's business, but my recommendation—and it's only a recommendation—is that you get moving."

CHAPTER 26

To demonstrate how much time was of the essence, I'm going to skip the part where we exchanged a few more lines of dialogue, left Esmeralda's House of Jewelry, had a wacky misadventure where we couldn't find the keys to the taxi, fought a bird (long story), got the cab in motion, discussed whether we should try to retrieve Mr. Click or the other doll first, decided on Mr. Click in a surprisingly unanimous decision, and drove toward the manhole where we would hopefully still find our history teacher.

"Why didn't you tell us?" I asked Adam.

"Tell you what?"

"That you got the voodoo doll for free because they think you're the Chosen One! We asked if you were keeping something from us. You said no. We asked again. You said no. We knew you were lying. Do you know how embarrassing it is to hear about this from a stranger?"

"I don't want to be the Chosen One," said Adam. "I mean, I don't even want to be a hall monitor, so how can I be responsible for saving humanity?"

"Well, if it makes you feel any better, she's clearly a raving lunatic."

"I don't know. I've always felt like I was meant for something important, something historic, but I thought maybe I'd become a famous singer or something. Remember that one song I wrote, where I tapped spoons on glasses? That was kind of catchy, right?"

"I don't remember it."

"It went 'La, la, la, tra la la, le la…' You really don't remember that? Oh well. Either way, I don't think Esmeralda is wrong about this."

"Oh, she's wrong."

"Stop being so blind, Tyler," said Kelley. "Nothing tonight can be explained by science. I tried, and I finally gave up. Obviously, Adam *does* impact magic in strange and unusual ways, and it's clearly his destiny to save us from the frickin' hobgoblins."

"All right, I was headed in that direction too. I was mostly arguing on your behalf."

"Do you think I should change my hair?" asked Adam.

"As the Chosen One, I'd think that you decide what is fashionable," I said. "So wear your hair however you want."

"I guess you're right. I wish somebody else was chosen. We should have asked to read the prophecies…maybe they say if you live through tonight or not."

"We'll find out soon." I was trying not to think about my potential fate. Despite living in Florida, I'd always been more of a cold weather guy, and I could never get behind the idea of eternal torment. I mean, by the fourth or fifth century of being endlessly hacked apart by rusty sabers, you'd be bored out of your mind.

Yeah, I'll admit it: I was terrified. No shame in that, right?

"Hey, there's that pay phone that I thought was the other pay phone," said Adam. "We're getting close."

I tried once again to maintain a positive attitude. Everything would be fine. Mr. Click had not been caught in a river of sewage and washed out into the ocean. His body had not been devoured by rats, forcing us to round up all of the individual rats that had him in their bellies. He had not sprouted tentacles and pulled himself miles away.

He'd be exactly where we left him. Perhaps gift-wrapped.

"Do you remember which one it was?" I asked.

Adam looked panicked. "Was I supposed to?"

"No," I said, sparing us the necessity of another madcap misadventure where we drove around in circles trying to find the right manhole cover. "It's a couple of blocks away."

The streets were still empty. This was good because we were about to do something that many people might find morally questionable but also bad because in our injured conditions it would've been nice to be able to say, "Hey, anybody wanna join us for a zombie-wrangling party?"

"There it is," I said.

Adam parked on the side of the street right next to it and shut off the engine. "I was going to try to lighten the mood by making a joke about how you owe me a fare," he said, "but then I thought, no, that's weak."

"It might have been funny."

"Should I do it now?"

"No."

We got out of the taxi and began the process of removing the manhole cover again, this time with a lot more urgency. At one point, we lost our grip on it, and it clanked down onto where two of my toes *would* have been, so in the end, everything, including bodily mutilation, happens for a reason.

"Do you see him?" I asked, peering down into the semidarkness.

"No," said Kelley.

We all listened closely for any zombie-esque sounds but heard nothing.

"I'll go," said Adam. "I'll find where he is, and then you guys can come down and help me bring him up."

"Are you supposed to be doing things like that?"

"I'm the only one who isn't hurt. Except for the marks on my chest, but those itch more than anything. It doesn't make sense for anybody else to go. I may be more important to the future than you two, but that doesn't mean I'm going to let you take all the risks."

He climbed down the ladder and disappeared from sight.

Then he screamed.

Then there was silence.

"Uh, Adam?" I called down.

Nothing.

Kelley and I looked at each other.

"Adam?" Kelley called down. "Are you okay?"

Still nothing.

"Okay, well, I guess we don't get to sit this one out," said Kelley.

"I'll go," I said. "I'm more used to my foot than you are your leg."

There was so much to be said, but I'd pretty much said it all that other time when I thought I might be headed toward certain death. I had no time to waste. I climbed down the ladder, walked forward several feet, and saw Adam's body.

I don't mean his dead body. I apologize for startling you if that's what you thought. He was lying on the ground (not in raw sewage or anything like that; it smelled nasty down here, but it was more of a rock tunnel than a river of poo).

Mr. Click was on top of him, hands sort of flopping around as if he was trying to get them around Adam's neck.

I hurried over there and shoved Mr. Click off of him. I quickly grabbed Adam's arms and dragged him back toward the ladder as Mr. Click scooted toward us, moving with surprising haste for somebody with no working arms and only one leg.

"Get back!" I said, kicking him in the face as hard as I could.

Mr. Click rolled onto his side and pulled himself into the fetal position. Adam coughed and rubbed his throat, even though he hadn't actually been strangled.

"How the hell did he get you?" I asked.

"I dunno. I guess I tripped over him."

Sometimes no rude comment can suffice, so I returned my attention to Mr. Click.

He looked sad.

Scared.

Like a wounded puppy.

"Mr. Click?"

He flinched at the sound of my voice.

"Mr. Click, I'm sorry I kicked you like that, but you sort of tried to strangle Adam, right?"

Why was I talking to him? I had a tight time frame to avoid lakes of fire!

He just looked so...*sad*.

"Don't go getting all sympathetic," I told him. "You were a creep. You made my life miserable. You falsely accused me of cheating."

Mr. Click's eyes had gone all teary.

"We never meant for this to happen. We just wanted your leg to hurt. I'm so sorry about what we did. It was an accident. Well, no, not an accident. It was on purpose, but we didn't think it would have anywhere near that much impact."

Mr. Click's mouth opened, as if he wanted to speak but couldn't. He was probably trying to assign us more homework.

"He looks sad," said Adam.

"I *know* he looks sad! What do you want me to do about that? I can't help it if he looks sad!"

Maybe Mr. Click wasn't such a bad teacher. Maybe everything he did was to encourage his students to achieve greatness. What if he'd gone home every night, sipped a cup of tea, and chuckled about how he was keeping those crazy kids on their toes? "Someday," he'd say, a warm smile on his face, "those kids will have jobs that they love and true inner happiness, and I'll have helped them, if only a little."

Or maybe he was an evil jerk.

Either way, my heart broke for this sorrowful, frightened, pathetic creature squirming around on the ground, even if he had just tried to strangle Adam.

"Maybe he wasn't such a bad teacher," said Adam. "He sort of inspired me to do better. I didn't *do* better, but there were lots of times where I thought I should. Maybe this was just his teaching style. When the gypsy lady mentioned Chef Ramsay, that made me think about all of those reality shows where the host is really mean to the contestants, but he's really just trying to make them be the best they can possibly be. And yeah, also to boost ratings, but I don't think Mr. Click would've cared about TV ratings. He was above that sort of thing."

"Can we get him out of here now?"

"Yeah, yeah. Sorry."

Kelley slowly came down the ladder, wincing with each step. "Ow," she said. "Ow," she said again. "Ow," she said once more. But it was a brave, strong "ow," not a whiny "ow." My admiration for my girlfriend knew no bounds. If it weren't for the fact that this relationship was always going to be a she-dumps-me-and-not-the-other-way-around type of deal, I would have known at that moment that I would never break up with her.

"Oh, good, he's right there," said Kelley. "Don't get me wrong, I think it's awful that his arms are broken and his leg is gone, but it does make him easy to keep track of."

"That's really morbid," I said. "But accurate."

Then Kelley looked the way she did when we went to see kittens at the humane society. "Oh, look at him. He looks so sad. I know you don't want to hear this right now, but I never thought he was all that mean."

"He was horrible!" I insisted.

"He was good at what he did. Maybe public speaking wasn't

really his thing, but he knew the information, and he could always answer questions, and I think he truly cared about each and every one of us."

"He hated us!"

"He hated it when we didn't apply ourselves. He hated it when we didn't strive for excellence. He hated when he didn't think we were being good citizens. But to him, there was no teacher's pet. We were all his pets."

"Oh, for God's sake…"

"I've never seen such sad, soulful eyes."

"I know," said Adam. "They're haunting."

"He was the best teacher we've ever had. No other teacher cared as much. After we get out of here, I'm going to start raising money for the Mr. Click Memorial Library. I think he'd like that."

"Or maybe you could put a bunch of books he liked on an e-reader," Adam suggested.

"That works too. But we have to do *something* to honor him."

"I miss him," said Adam. "Even though he's right there, I miss him. When you stop and think about it, who is the real monster: the mean history teacher or the kids who turned him into a broken zombie? It's gonna be hard for me to face the mirror for a while."

"Can we please *get* him *up* the *ladder* before I *burn in hell*?" I asked.

"Oh yeah," said Adam. "Sorry."

"Well, well, well," said a familiar voice. It was not Kelley, and it was not Adam, and it was not Mr. Click. It also wasn't Zeke,

Mildred, Glenn, Franklin, Donna, or Donnie. (Donnie was that guy from the beginning who cheated off my test, whom I confronted at his locker but he wouldn't admit it.)

It was Ribeye.

He was pointing a gun at me.

"Man, I've been walking around these tunnels forever. I didn't expect to find you again."

"Shouldn't you have just gone up the ladder to the junkyard?" I asked. "That's where I left you."

"I would have done that, except I wandered around in a daze for a while. You busted my head up pretty good. I haven't forgotten that."

"Your gun's empty," I said.

Ribeye shook his head. "I had an extra clip in my pocket."

"Prove it—no, no, don't prove it. What do you want?"

"What do you think I want?"

"Peace for all?"

"Not quite." He looked down at Mr. Click. "You really messed this dude up. What'd he do to you?"

"Nothing. It never should have happened."

"Maybe I'll put a mercy bullet in his head after I kill you," said Ribeye. He squeezed the trigger.

And then Adam jumped in front of me.

CHAPTER 27

Adam was not quick enough. The bullet sailed past him.

And past me.

And hit Kelley in the chest.

She fell to the ground.

Ribeye squeezed off another shot. Adam tried to dive in front of this one as well but missed again, and this bullet nicked my shoulder.

It felt like a mosquito bite delivered by an eight-hundred-pound mosquito.

Ribeye was about to fire a third shot, but then Mr. Click grabbed his foot.

"Oh, you want to play, huh?" asked Ribeye, grinning. "Play with this."

He fired into Mr. Click's back.

Ribeye's grin vanished.

"You're supposed to let go when I shoot you!" He shot Mr. Click in the back again. Then in the head. Mr. Click did not release his foot. "Hey, this ain't right!"

Adam rushed at him, tackling Ribeye to the ground. Another gunshot went off, hitting the stone ceiling.

Kelley lay on her side, with a lot of blood on her shirt. I rushed over and crouched down next to her.

"Help Adam," she wheezed.

Adam punched Ribeye in the face, but it was an Adam-quality punch and didn't have much effect. I don't know if zombies have adrenaline, but Mr. Click seemed to have a rush of it, and even though three of his four major appendages weren't in working order and an alarming portion of his skull was now gone, he made his way over to the Adam/Ribeye fight.

He butted his head against Adam, pushing him off the thug and leaving a small brain stain on Adam's shirt.

Then Mr. Click pounced on Ribeye.

This next part is gross.

He dug his teeth into Ribeye's neck and...well, let's just say that it wasn't a sensual vampire bite. He swallowed without sufficiently chewing it up and then took another bite. And then a third bite, munching as quickly as a contestant in a hot dog–eating contest.

At this point, I realized that this was pretty much the end of poor Ribeye. So I focused entirely on Kelley.

"Does it hurt?" I asked her, tears streaming down my face.

"Yes."

"That's a good sign, though, isn't it? It's when it stops hurting that you're in trouble."

"No, it hurts like a [bleep]."

"Good."

"I'm sorry I can't..." She paused to cough up some blood. "I'm sorry I can't help you...get Mr. Click up the...ladder."

"You can't die on me," I said. "I won't let you."

"Oh my God!" Adam screamed. "He just bit off his nose!"

"I may not...be dying," said Kelley.

"Do you feel like you want to say, 'So cold, so cold?'"

"No."

"Maybe you'll be okay."

"Oh my God!" Adam screamed. "He just bit off a bunch of the flesh that had been around his nose!"

"Adam..." said Kelley. "...come here..."

Adam hurried over and crouched down on the other side of Kelley. "You're going to be okay," he told her. "I promise."

"I need you...to help Tyler."

"I will. I will."

"I'm not going to...die...quite yet." She coughed again. "I've got...more time than...Tyler does. Leave me here. Get the other doll."

"I'm not leaving you here," I said.

"Then you're...going to hell...dumbass."

"Hell is worse than dying in a sewer," said Adam. "Let's get moving."

I gave Kelley a tender kiss on the lips. "We'll be back."

"If you...think you'll...be...gone...for more than...let's say...forty-five minutes...call an ambulance."

"We will," I promised. "Are you sure you're okay being down here with Ribeye? He's really unpleasant to look at."

"I'll...close my eyes."

Adam and I pulled Mr. Click off Ribeye's body. Mr. Click looked at us, and for a moment, I could see the humanity beneath the surface, as if his eyes were saying, *That was for you. Now solve your problem so you can go on to live a long, happy life.*

"How are we going to get him up there?" I asked.

"Well, we know he's okay with being shot in the head," said Adam. "If we cut him in two, we could each take half up the ladder."

"First let's see if there's a rope in the cab."

There was indeed a rope in the trunk of the cab. That surprised me. I have no idea why it was there; honestly, I only threw that suggestion out there so we could say we tried another option before we sawed Mr. Click in half.

We tied one end of the rope around Mr. Click's waist and the other end to the back of the taxi. Adam drove forward, raising his body, and yeah, it smacked the top of the manhole pretty darn hard, but it was still the least messy alternative.

We put his body in the trunk.

"I'll be back soon!" I called down.

We got in the cab and sped off.

"Do you think she's going to be okay?" Adam asked.

I nodded. "Yeah. She's strong."

"Do you think her parents are going to be mad that we left her bleeding in the sewer?"

"She's going to be fine. Look, Adam, I just want to say that even though the bullet missed you and hit her, I appreciate that you tried to take a bullet for me."

"That's what friends do, right?"

"Yeah, I guess you're right. Thank you."

"No need to thank me. If the bullet had hit me, he still had other bullets, and he would've just shot you and Kelley right after my sacrifice. The real person you should thank is Mr. Click."

I turned around and looked at the backseat, which was as close as I could get to seeing the trunk. "Thanks, Mr. Click."

"Do you think things are going to change for us?" Adam asked.

"I would say yes."

"I hope they don't."

"We'll find out pretty soon."

We were astonished that the only thing that went wrong during the drive was that we stopped at a red light and some guy got in the back of the cab and told us to take him to the airport. But then he saw my ear and said that he'd find another cab.

As we turned into my neighborhood, I said, "You've got to do this. If I go in there, they'll never let me leave."

"Okay. Where's the doll?"

"Under my bed. It's in the same box."

"All right. Should I pretend that I don't know where you are, or should I make up some cover story about how you were kidnapped and how I need the box to fill a ransom demand?"

"Maybe you should just say, 'Trust me, I'll explain everything later,' and not get into specifics. Be smooth."

"Smooth. I can do that."

As we turned onto my block, I could see that a police car was parked outside of my house. That was better than having three or four police cars parked out there. It meant that maybe the cops were there for the missing teenager and not the gang slayings and the escaped cadaver and stuff.

"Stop a couple of houses away so they don't see the car," I said.

Adam turned off the engine. "Wish me luck."

"Good luck."

"Remember, smooth."

"Smooth as silk."

"Yes."

"Smooth as chocolate."

"Let it go, Adam."

"One doll, coming up," he said, getting out of the car. "Smooth. Smooooooooth."

He jogged toward my house.

This would work out. He'd get the doll, and we'd be on our way. I checked my watch. We still had about…oh crap, only twenty minutes. I'd have to violate the occasional traffic law.

It would be fine. It would be fine.

And if not, how bad could hell really be? No doubt it was exaggerated for publicity purposes.

Adam knocked on my front door and then walked inside.

Sure, he'd be swarmed with questions, but I'm sure he'd handle the situation with the utmost smoothness, and he'd just stroll right out with the doll tucked under his arm.

Maybe the taxi should be closer to the house just in case.

I scooted into the driver's seat and drove the car in front of my home. I knew that my mom and dad were suffering, and I felt terrible about it, but there was no time to explain. I could imagine the conversation.

Me: Mom! Dad! I'm alive!

Mom: Oh, thank goodness! We're so relieved! Uh, where did you get that taxi?

Me: No time to explain! I have to go! Quickly!

Dad: No! We can't let you out of our sight! Not after fearing we'd lost you forever!

Police Officer #1: You need to answer some questions for us first, young man.

Me: If I don't get to Esmeralda's House of Jewelry in the next twenty minutes, somebody will die!

Police Officer #2: Oh no! It's our job to stop people from dying! Hop into our police car, and we'll drive you right where you need to go, siren wailing and red-and-blue lights flashing! We'll get you there in time!

Me: Is there any chance that I could move something from the taxi's trunk to your trunk without you watching?

Police Officer #1: Probably not.

Me: What if I said I needed to bring along the body of that teacher who died today, and you could see the inside of his head?

Police Officer #2: We would take you into custody immediately.

Police Officer #1: And then we'd take you into an interrogation room and shine a bright light into your face, and one of us would pretend to be nice and the other one would pretend to be mean, and we'd ask you if you knew how much trouble you were in.

Police Officer #2: Then we'd break your fingers, one by one, until you talked.

Police Officer #1 [*to Officer #2*]: No, we wouldn't.

Police Officer #2: Well, don't tell *him* that!

Police Officer #1: Broken fingers or not, I assure you that if you involve your parents and the authorities, it would be extremely difficult to get permission to bring Mr. Click's body to the voodoo shop, and you wouldn't be able to convince us to let you drive the cab with a police escort either, because why would it be so important that you drive that specific cab? Doesn't make sense. Not gonna happen.

The front door of my house flew open, and Adam came running out, followed by my mom.

"*Drive! Drive! Drive!*"

CHAPTER 28

[Email address withheld.]

Hi, Tyler! It's your friendly editor here! I just read Chapter 28 of your book, and all I can say is, WOW!!! The whole time I was reading the book, I was thinking, "How in the world is he going to top the awesome stuff that's happened before?" but you went and did it!

Amazing. Best car chase ever.

Honestly, if I didn't know that this story was completely true, I'm not sure I'd believe it. You've got Adam running out of your house with your parents *and* two police officers following, and then right in the middle of this pulse-pounding action, there was that moment where you see the tears in your mother's eyes and...oh, the amount of emotion you packed into just twelve paragraphs was unbelievable!

Then that whole chase, where Adam can't get

into the car but jumps up onto the hood, and then your mom *almost gets the back door open* so you had to speed off. I kept saying out loud, "Oh my God! Oh my God!" My husband kept asking what was wrong, and I kept reading him parts of the book, and then *he* started saying, "Oh my God! Oh my God!" If you don't win the Pulitzer Prize for this, then the Pulitzer committee should all go drown themselves in a swimming pool with extra chlorine. That's all I've got to say about that.

(Don't tell the Pulitzer committee I said that! LOL!)

So then you're speeding off, and the cops rush back to their cars, and I'm thinking, "Oh, no way is Tyler ever going to get away with this! He's only sixteen! How can a sixteen-year-old beat two trained cops in a high-speed chase?" Yeah, the two cops were in the same vehicle, but still!

Wow! Did I say wow already? Wow! The excitement! The close calls! I thought Adam was dead for sure when you rolled down the window and he had to climb in at ninety miles per hour, and then that other car almost sideswiped you guys! How close did Adam come to getting crushed between the vehicles? Inches?

And then you swerved into the wrong lane against oncoming traffic! No, wait...that's part of my notes. I know this story is true, but it would be really cool if you swerved into the wrong lane against oncoming traffic and had to dodge a whole bunch of cars. Come on, one little exaggeration won't get you in trouble. Do it for me? Thanks! Love ya.

The roadblock scene. I don't want to be repetitious, but wow. Wow, wow, wow. That was crazy! My favorite part was how after not using actual profanity through the whole book, you went ahead and put the s-word in there. You managed to give the s-word its power again. Amazing.

Oh, and I loved how all of those cop cars got destroyed but no cops actually got hurt. I would have lost sympathy for you and Adam if you'd caused any police officers to die or be seriously injured. (They do have families after all). But no, it was just property destruction!

And then...how many cop cars were chasing you guys? Eight? I was on the edge of my seat, reading that. I mean, literally on the edge of my seat. My husband kept saying, "You're going to fall off the chair if you don't scoot back a little," and I kept saying, "I can't! I can't!"

I don't know about the part where the earth cracked open and you had to drive around the cracks. I looked it up, and apparently the earth *did* crack open like you said, but that's where you started to lose me a little. Maybe tone it down just a notch.

Also, the helicopter. That part was kind of dumb.

And there's a continuity error where you've been driving, but then suddenly Adam is driving with no explanation. Why did you guys change drivers? How did you do it when you were driving so fast? Clearly there's a logical explanation for this, but it's not in the book itself, so when I read that, I went, "Whoa! What's up with *that*?" and it kind of took me out of the story. Was the taxi almost out of fuel, so you had to quickly pull into a gas station, and maybe Adam scooted over into the driver's seat while you pumped the gas? Again, I don't want you to lie about anything, but gas station scene = potential for huge explosion. Think about it.

Oh, but I did like how we then found out that Adam had told the cops where Kelley was before he ran out of your house. That was nice, because during the whole car chase, I was thinking, "This is really exciting, but they should have said something to the cops so they could send an ambulance over to help that poor girl." What if you moved that piece a little earlier? Otherwise the reader is going, "Why should I care about this awesome six-car pileup when Kelley is bleeding to death?"

And then you turned onto Duncan Street, and your stomach started to hurt...almost like it was burning. Wow.

That was the best final action sequence I've

ever read in a book. I was stunned. If you were dangling from a cliff, and William Shakespeare was dangling from the same cliff, and I only had time to save one of you, it would be, "Sorry, Bill, looks like you're plummeting to your death!"

Everybody in the office agreed that you deserve twice as much money for this book. Check your PayPal account!

Anyway, the reason I'm writing is that I accidentally deleted the file with Chapter 28, and I know you'd mentioned that you were having computer problems, so hopefully you had a backup.

Ciao!

Love, Mindy

[Email address withheld.]

Dear Mindy,

Crap.

Sincerely, Tyler

CHAPTER 29

I grimaced.

"What's wrong?" Adam asked.

"My stomach hurts all of a sudden."

"Like how? Like you ate a jalapeno?"

"Way worse than that. It's like a battery acid capsule just broke in there."

"That's not good. So it's an incineration-from-within kind of feeling?"

"Yeah. *Ow! Crap!* My stomach is sizzling!"

Adam floored the accelerator, driving even faster than he had when we outran all of those police cars.

"Please hurry," I said. "I don't wanna burn!"

"You're not gonna burn. Just stay with me. Be a rock. We're almost there. Life is good. Stay happy. Almost there. Almost there. Keep being a rock. Almost there. Damn, just passed it. Backing up."

He stopped the cab. We threw open the doors and hurried to the back. My stomach gave another intense jolt of pain, and I fell to my knees.

"No! Don't give up!" Adam shouted. "We're almost safe! Look how close we...oh crap, the trunk is locked."

He ran back to the front of the taxi and returned a few seconds later with the keys. I managed to stand up as we unlocked the trunk, threw open the lid, and frantically pulled out Mr. Click.

We lost our grip, and he fell onto the ground.

There was thin white smoke in the air, which I realized was coming from my nostrils.

"That's not good. That's not good, but just stay calm, stay calm," said Adam. "Maybe they can come to us." He rushed over to the door of the voodoo shop and turned the knob. "It's locked! They closed on us!" He rapped on the door, then kicked it a couple of times.

Smoke was billowing from my nostrils and my mouth. My stomach felt like a little pyromaniac was inside there, lighting matches and giggling.

Adam ran back to the cab, reached inside the trunk, and grabbed a tire iron.

The smoke was starting to turn black.

Adam shattered the front window of the store. An alarm went off.

Esmeralda peeked her head out. I could see that she was holding my doll. "Why the hell you break window? I on my way!"

A flame came out of one of my nostrils. It was just a tiny flame, but still, fire was never supposed to come out of your nose!

Adam tossed Mr. Click's doll to Esmeralda.

Esmeralda raised both dolls into the air. "*Uiptf jo dibshf pg tvdi uijoht, dbodfm uijt tqfmm jg zpv xpvme!*" (I don't know how she pronounced the words without vowels either.)

The smoke disappeared.

My stomach stopped hurting.

Mr. Click gave me one last sad look, and then he closed his eyes.

"He at peace now," said Esmeralda. "Doll's power is gone." She ripped off the head of my doll. "See?"

"I…I…I…hold on a second. Let me catch my breath… Okay…no, wait, haven't caught it yet." I stood there for a long moment, trying to regain my composure. Adam patted me on the back. "I don't know how to thank you," I said.

Esmeralda took me by the hand and stared deep into my eyes. "You have responsibility now. Serious responsibility. You tell tale of Chosen One. You write it so future generations know of glory of Adam Westell. You write it good, not mess up. Find publisher. This your destiny."

"I accept," I said.

"You no have choice, but is good that you accept."

"So, about the corpse," I said. "Do you need us to take it away and figure out what to do with it, or will you take care of it?"

"We handle."

"Thanks. Adam, any chance you could take me to the hospital?"

"Sure thing."

CHAPTER 367

Yeah, I'm fudging a bit on the chapter numbers, but think how impressed people will be when you tell them you've just finished a book with 367 chapters!

Anyway, this is the part of the book where we wrap things up. [*Denouement.*] First of all, Kelley did not die. Adam's directions were superb, and the paramedics found her down there in plenty of time to save her life. I'm not saying that they just slapped a Band-Aid on her and she was fine—there was a lengthy hospital stay involved and some rehab and a scar that I can't convince her looks really cool—but now she's fine.

I, too, spent some time in the hospital. I wish I could talk about the miracles of modern science and how they synthesized replacement flesh for me, but no, I still only have eight toes, and my ear didn't grow back. When I get bummed out about it, I remind myself that it could have been much worse.

Kelley, Adam, and I decided that instead of getting trapped in a web of lies, we would tell the truth about everything, no matter how bizarre the truth might be. The police did not believe us. It didn't help that Esmeralda's House of

Jewelry had magically covered their tracks, even repairing the broken glass, and denied all knowledge of doing business with us.

There were investigations out the wazoo and lots of press coverage, and many experts weighed in on how a dead body could go missing from the morgue and why the security camera footage from that evening was too blurry to see and why there was no DNA evidence from our history teacher in the sewer, trunk of the taxi, or sidewalk. One expert said, "I think it *is* magic!" but he was not taken seriously by his colleagues.

The dead thugs in the garage thing kept coming up, but because they didn't believe in the voodoo doll, ultimately, the authorities decided that I was just stupid enough to risk my life to get my mom's car back. Ribeye's death was indeed ruled an act of cannibalism, but without a cannibal available to match the dental marks, there wasn't much they could do.

The Basers all went to prison, because freedom of religion does not include the right to conduct human sacrifices in your home.

Zeke, the cabdriver, was never found. He's probably still lurking out there…somewhere…perhaps watching you at this very moment.

Regarding the algebra equation of how mad my parents would be, it was about two weeks of "Oh, we're so glad to have our precious little boy back!" and then about two months of "You will *suffer* for the emotional trauma you inflicted upon us!" My mom did eventually get her car back, though.

The investigation kept going on and on, but then I started noticing tall men in black suits hanging around, looking stern, and then the mayor announced that the investigation into the strange events surrounding the death of Mr. Click was being concluded and that everything had been officially ruled a tragic accident. I don't know what that's about.

Adam and I are still friends. After his initial reluctance, he started to get an ego about the whole Chosen One thing, but I put a stop to that.

Then there was an extremely awkward misunderstanding where I thought Kelley was developing a crush on him because of the whole Chosen One thing, but I had merely misinterpreted some signals, and it was all very embarrassing, and we worked it out.

Our new history teacher, Mr. Venison, was *way* meaner than Mr. Click.

And, well, I guess that's it for now. Things have settled down, and I'm getting good grades, and I'm starting to think about college. So thanks for reading. I apologize if there were any grammar issues. I hope you liked the book, and until more weird stuff starts to happen that I need to write about, "All Hail He Who Shall Save Us from the Hobgoblins."

COMING SOON...

A Bad Day for Witchcraft
A Bad Day for Sorcery
A Bad Day for Necromancy
A Bad Day for Hypnosis
A Bad Day for Levitation
A Bad Day for Astral Projection
A Bad Day for Snake Charming
A Bad Day for Demonic Possession
A Bad Day for Cryogenics
A Bad Day for Ventriloquism
A Bad Day for Yoga
A Bad Day for Voodoo II
A Bad Day for Drinking Poison
A Good Day for Dancing
A Bad Day for Shameless Cash-Ins
A Bad Day for Voodoo 3-D
A Bad Day for Eating Stuff off the Ground
A Bad Day for That Guy Who's About to Be Hit by a Bus
A Bad Day for Slugs

A Bad Day for Voodoo (rewrite)

A Bad Day for Nudity

A Bad Day for the Olympics

A Mediocre Day for Walking

A Bad Day for Taxation without Representation

A Bad Day for Lady Gaga

A Bad Day for Voodoo II (rewrite)

Harry Potter v. A Bad Day for Voodoo

A Bad Day for Licorice

A Bad Day for Taunting Llamas

A Bad Day for Sequels

Are you still reading?

Ummmm…I'm out of story. Sorry. I assumed that everybody would have given up by now. I've said everything I wanted to say, and yeah, I guess I failed to fully explore a thematic element or two, but that was on purpose.

Hmm. Maybe you have a younger brother or sister who wants to read this book, but as a responsible older sibling, you've said "NO!!! There's too much blood! You'll have nightmares!" In that case, let's give them something they can read!

Riddle: How do you make a voodoo doll float?

Answer: Two scoops of ice cream, some root beer, and a voodoo doll!

Actually, I think voodoo dolls float anyway. At least the ones made out of light fabric do. But it's still kind of a funny riddle, right?

Okay, look, this book wasn't meant for your little brother or sister. If they're all like "Lemme read it! Lemme read it!" tell them that they have to wait until they're old enough to think that people losing body parts is funny, because that's basically the whole book.

Oh…one more thing. Did you leave a five-star review online to help balance out all the one-star reviews this thing is going to get? That would be appreciated. I mean, don't lie in your review or anything like that, but feel free to exaggerate. If you thought it was only three stars, maybe you were tired and had other things on your mind while you were reading it, and you didn't truly appreciate every little nuance, like that part where I was talking to the Rottweiler. There is so much nuance in that scene that you wouldn't even believe all of it if I told you.

I'm not asking you to commit fraud on online review sites. Certainly not. I'm just saying that if you didn't think this book deserves five stars out of five, you might have been too worried about global warming to fully concentrate.

Your call. No pressure.

Anyway, the book is over now. Move along. Go read *A Confederacy of Dunces*.

ACKNOWLEDGMENTS

No book is the work of just one person. You need other people to tell you which parts you messed up. So, in alphabetical order by last name, because that's the way I roll, thank you to Tod Clark, Lynne Hansen, Leah Hultenschmidt, Adrienne Jones, Michael McBride, Jim Morey, Rick Moschgat, Shane Ryan Staley, Rhonda Wilson, and Kristin Zelazko for their sharp, cruel eyes.

ABOUT THE AUTHOR

Jeff Strand is the author of a bunch of books. Most of them are meant to be funny. He lives in Tampa, Florida, and doesn't believe in voodoo, though he still thinks you should carry a doll around, go up to people you don't like, and chuckle while you jab it with pins just to make them squirm. Poke around his gleefully macabre website at www.jeffstrand.com.